3/01

Wall Street Wizard

Wall Street Wizard

SOUND IDEAS FROM A SAVVY TEEN INVESTOR

Jay Liebowitz

Simon & Schuster Books for Young Readers
New York   London   Toronto   Sydney   Singapore

Dedicated to my wonderful parents, Jack and Carolyn, and my
two furry siblings, Mackie and Piper

ACKNOWLEDGEMENTS

Many people have helped with this book. Without their aid, it
would have never reached its final form. I'd like to thank David
Gale, the editor who approached me with the idea, as well as
John Rudolph, his assistant; and Karen Blumenthal, who gave
me solid evidence that I wasn't as smart about stocks as I
thought. Warren Buffett must also receive his fair share of credit;
if he hadn't been such an excellent investor, I wouldn't have had
an early path to follow. And finally, I must thank my parents:
Carolyn, who taught me to love books and to be my own man,
and Jack, who, with his fairness and humor, showed me how.

SIMON & SCHUSTER BOOKS FOR YOUNG READERS
An imprint of Simon & Schuster Children's Publishing Division
1230 Avenue of the Americas, New York, New York 10020
Text copyright © 2000 by Jay Liebowitz
All rights reserved including the right of reproduction in whole
or in part in any form.
SIMON & SCHUSTER BOOKS FOR YOUNG READERS is a trademark of Simon & Schuster.
Book design by Joyce White. The text for this book is set in Cheltenham book.
Printed in the United States of America
10 9 8 7 6 5 4 3 2 1
Library of Congress Cataloging-in-Publication Data
Liebowitz, Jay.
Wall Street wizard : sound ideas from a savvy teen investor / by Jay Liebowitz.
p. cm.
ISBN 0-689-83401-2
1. Investments—Handbooks, manuals, etc. 2. Teenagers—Finance, Personal—
Handbooks, manuals, etc.
HG4527.L53 2000
00-032931

FIRST
EDITION

Contents

Hitch your wagon to a star.
—Ralph Waldo Emerson

Introduction

I never gave Wall Street a second thought until I was thirteen. I'd heard about the Dow in the news, but who ever bothered with that stuff? That was for my mother and father, and at some point I expected that they'd give me some kind of pep talk in which they'd tell me all the secrets of making and investing money. That never happened, but one day I stumbled across a book on investing, and it opened a whole new world.

My first breakthrough came around my thirteenth birthday. I was ever the entrepreneur, even though I wanted badly to be a doctor, and I was preparing to sell a computer software program I had developed. For a couple of years, I had programmed software with a very easy software editing program. While making the software required creativity here and there, I was more interested in cranking out something that I could sell over an on-line service. When I finally finished the program, it was massive—several hundred kilobytes. Before super-fast Internet connections, downloading the program took almost an hour. But I was one of the lucky few software programmers, and the product sold. At this point, I knew I wanted to do something in business, but I only had a vague idea of what. Meanwhile, I told everybody else that I was set on becoming a surgeon. That dream was gradually falling to pieces.

Then one day I was fishing around at the library, probably searching for an anatomy book or some other kind of biology book, and for the fun of it, I decided to pick out an investment book. It wasn't thick—that was a good sign. The jacket promised that I could "invest [my] money, and never work again." Well, I had never worked, except at cranking out a software program, and so something that promised to give me enough money to retire before I even started seemed like something great!

In fact, I never knew that individual investors, people like my parents, could make money in the stock market (I quickly learned the stock market was on Wall Street)—not just a few bucks, but *a lot* of money. I not only read that book, I picked out a new one every time I went to the library. Soon there wasn't a book on the shelf I hadn't read. I went online to the Internet and started looking at books reviewed at Amazon.com. I went to the library catalog and reserved books to read about stocks. I read the classics. I read the not-so-classics. I read the get-rich-quick books and the ones that say getting rich takes two lifetimes.

This was my passion, but I knew it wasn't shared by everybody. I don't know why, but stocks just "feel" bad to some people. Maybe it's because they require simple math or because stocks don't offer a 100% guarantee of making money. But life is full of risk. Why don't you pay somebody to get your paper in the morning, since there isn't a *100%* guarantee that you'll make it to the curb without getting attacked by a roving dog? You don't pay someone because that's the nature of life. Young investors can reduce some of the risk by learning and the golden advantage of time. I started a web site, the Wall Street Wizard (www.streetwhiz.com), to help young investors understand this principle.

Learning to invest takes time, and the earlier you enter the game, the easier it becomes. If you're a basketball player, try playing against a guy who has been playing for thirty years. Even though you're younger and more agile, he's got the moves and skill of a person with experience. If you keep investing, after thirty years you'll be able to knock the socks off anyone who starts at forty or fifty. And you'll be richer.

So start now. Don't worry if you make a few errors when you begin. Keep the faith. Investing can be fun, exciting, and even easy. If you like to make money, this book can be your guide. This book isn't about getting rich quick, nor is it about being a miser and leaving a gigantic fortune. It's somewhere in between—between a fast fortune and one you'll never enjoy—a mix of intelligence and caution. If you know something about investing now, I guarantee that you will learn more. If you know nothing, by the time you finish you'll be on the path to becoming a Wall Street wizard.

Here's what you'll learn:

- The basics: An overview of Wall Street lingo and what it means.
- Sources of information: How to get ideas and information from television, radio, and the Internet.
- Financial planning: Exactly what to do with your college or job money, even if you have only a small amount.
- Where to trade: How to set up an account with only a little money and pay next to nothing in commissions.
- Great ideas for investing.
- How you can make money by ignoring what everybody else says.
- Secrets to consistent profits, year after year.
- Investing for the future—learn to earn now and never worry about money later.
- What the best books are to help you learn as rapidly as possible.

Right now, lots of people are making money in the stock market. You can, too. The secret is consistency. The stock market is like working out: To improve your heart and live longer, you can't work out intensely just one day a week. The same is true for making money in the market: It takes years of consistent efforts to make incredible amounts of money.

I want to teach you the secrets of money. Don't be fooled. There aren't any quick and easy ways to get rich, but there are intelligent and fun ways. And there are also tricks. For example, have you ever heard your parents talk about the IRS, which is the Internal Revenue Service—the government organization that collects those dreadful taxes? Well, I can teach you a thing or two about keeping your contribution to the government low. I can teach you the five principles that all wealthy people understand. And in the end, we'll talk about some interesting things that you can read more about—like other methods of investing.

Money is important, and it's difficult to understand. But it's not impossible. Do your best. Read this book. Reread it. Read other books. Before you know it, you'll be a Wall Street wizard and teaching me a thing or two. Good luck, and I wish you the best on your road to knowledge.

Jay Liebowitz
September 2000

PART I

Getting a Jump on the Street

Money Made Easy

I've seen the movie *Wall Street* five times. Now, I don't pride myself on being the type who waits in line for hours to see a movie on its opening day; but I do like movies, and I grew up in Los Angeles, the capital of the entertainment culture. Still, you have to agree that many kids would think it's weird to be fascinated with *Wall Street*. Most of my friends have never even heard of the movie.

What's more, the plot of the movie isn't all that attention-grabbing. It's about a stock broker who falls into the world of greed and deception in New York. If you've never seen this movie, go out and rent it. That's not a request, it's a command. It teaches the truth about investing, which is that we aren't here for our health or our brains, we're here for our wallets.

But you may finish watching the movie and say, "Look at all the problems Gekko created. Greed can't be good." I can just as easily point to the story of a Zen monk in a town in the East. Everyone thought he was a greedy monk. Every time there was a donation, he was the first in line to get it. If there were coins on the street, he picked them up. Then one day there was a major storm, and the town was all but destroyed. When the people woke up, there were carts, oxen, food, and supplies at the center of the city. The monk had furnished them all. The monk had had a vision about the destruction of the town, and his sole purpose in collecting the money was to help its inhabitants. Does this prove greed is good? No!

Greed is neither good nor bad, so long as you don't hurt people to get your money, and do help people once you've got it. So don't feel bad if you want money or you want more money than you have now. Just keep your greed in check. Gekko fell from grace because he sacrificed everything—his moral values, his happiness, his wife—for money. This isn't a book about philosophy, it's a book about money. Yet too many times I get messages from people who have suffered because they were too attached to their money. The wise man (and woman) knows: Money comes, money goes.

Okay, I'm sure you wouldn't say no to millions of dollars. But think about what you really want out of life. Do you want to learn about money so you can make a fortune? Or do you want to learn about money so you don't have to think about it? It's okay to be one or the other, or in between for that matter. Let's start with your situation now. You've opened this book, which means you think about money at least a little bit. If you're an average teenager, you make money doing different things. You may have a part-time job, you may do chores for other people, or you may just be lucky enough to be handed money by your parents. For many teenagers, that can add up to $50, even $100 a week. The average family makes a lot more: $500 a week. And the more you want, the more you can make. Doctors make an average of $2,000 a week. That's a lot of money, and it could pave the road to a very enjoyable retirement, which is having the option of quitting work and doing what you want to do.

In the past, people relied on the government to make payments to them when they hit age sixty-five. These payments were called **Social Security**, monthly payments made to retired persons from a Social Security fund, one for which the government draws money from every worker's check. When Social Security began, the government didn't believe that people would be living well past sixty-five. And the government has been stealing from the cookie jar—tapping the fund to balance the budget. Experts expect the fund to eventually go bankrupt, and one of the major issues in the 2000 presidential election is saving Social Security. The moral of the story: Don't bet on the government to be there for you. Bet on yourself. You can pave your own road to riches. But there's a big *IF*. That's *if* you learn to plan your financial future, to invest. The most annoyingly true cliché I've heard is, "Those who fail to plan, plan to fail."

So let's dive in and explore some of the ideas that form the basis of investing and building wealth. Let's talk about the first, perhaps most fundamental aspect of life. It's called **risk**. Risk has a certain negative connotation. People don't like it. And that's why many are stuck in jobs they don't like and in lives they hate: they refuse to take risks. But taking a risk doesn't mean laying it all on the line and going for broke. It doesn't mean betting it all on one hand.

Actually, taking manageable risks is something we do every day. You're taking a risk right now by reading this book. Maybe you'll finish it and decide that investing isn't your cup of tea, that reading this was a waste of time. If that's the case, you'll be able to move on. That's a manageable risk. The other possibility is that this book may motivate you to begin investing, which over your lifetime could enrich you by thousands of times the cost of this book. Overall, that's a wise risk.

Risk can be applied to every aspect of life, especially investing. Investing is the art of putting up money now to get more money in the future. That money you get is considered your **return on investment (ROI)**. There are tons of real-world examples of this. One of the most common is the money you put in the bank.

Let's say you put $10,000 in a bank tomorrow. The bank is willing to give you a 3% return on investment compounded yearly. That means this time next year you'll have $10,300, your original $10,000 plus an extra $300. If you don't touch the money, you'll have 3% more than that amount the following year. That means you'll have $10,609. Let's do the math:

Money put in the bank, the deposit: $10,000
Return on investment: 3.0% = 0.03
Calculate the return: $10,000 X 0.03 = $300 + $10,000 = $10,300
The next year, if you keep the money: $10,300 X 0.03 = $309 + $10,300 = $10,609

The wonderful thing is that if you don't touch your money it will grow faster and faster. In fact, at 3%, it can double within twenty-four years. Wow! Twenty-four years may seem like forever. You'll be an adult before $10,000 becomes $20,000. That may seem outrageously slow if you had ten thousand dollars, but if you could double a million dollars, that *would* be a lot of money. And if you received a rate of return higher than 3%, you could double your money even faster.

Doubling your money that quickly is an example of **compound interest**, the idea that you get a return on investment not only on the money that you initially put in (the principal) but also on the interest

YR	10% (ROI)	15%	20%	25%	30%
1	$55,000.00	$57,500.00	$60,000.00	$62,500.00	$65,000.00
5	$80,525.50	$100,567.86	$124,416.00	$152.587.89	$185,646.50
10	$129,687.12	$202,277.89	$309,586.82	$465,661.29	$689,292.46
15	$208,862.41	$406,853.08	$770,351.09	$1,421,085.47	$2,559,294.65
20	$336,374.99	$818,326.87	$1,916,879.99	$4,336,808.69	$9,502,481.89
25	$541,735.30	$1,645,947.63	$4,769,810.83	$13,234,889.80	$35,282,050.07
30	$872,470.11	$3,310,588.60	$11,868,815.69	$40,389,678.35	$130,999,782.18

from the principal. In other words, you get interest on interest. We'll talk about compound interest in detail later, but let's take the idea of ROI one step further. Why would a bank or anyone else want to pay you that extra $300 the first year? You're getting paid because you're giving the bank money now, allowing them to use it, and betting that they'll pay you back with even more. You're taking a risk, although a really small one. Your deposits are federally insured by the government up to $100,000 now, but at one time that wasn't the case. Banks were a far riskier place to put your money.

Risk is everywhere. Suppose you're not happy putting your money in the bank. Instead of putting it in the bank, which virtually guarantees you $300, you hear about some other investment which offers you $1000. Naturally, there's a lot more risk in investing in that.

As an investor, you're on a mission. Your mission is to get the best ROI possible. And the way to achieve that is to think of money in terms of ROI. In fact, ROI—we'll call it Roy—is my best friend. He stays with me whenever I'm shopping for a good investment, and I've never stopped looking for a **wealth-building return**. That's a return on your investment that allows your money to grow quickly and allows you to become *really* wealthy—while doing virtually nothing. We talked about a bank account with a 3% return yearly. Three percent is pathetic compared to the other possibilities. A good return is 15%. A great return is 25% or higher. With those returns, the money pyramids on itself. With a 25% return, an initial $10,000 investment becomes $12,500 in the first year. The next year that grows to $15,625. That growth continues and continues. Look at the table on this page to see how $50,000 grows. Match up the ROI and the number of years to see what a wonder compound interest is.

Beginning with $50,000, the investor receiving only a 10% return each year can end up with nearly $900,000 after the thirtieth year. At 20%, the investor can end up with $11 million, more than enough to retire rich.

Notice in the table that between the twentieth year and the thirtieth year the money really starts expanding quickly. Even earning a paltry 10% a year, you make over $500,000 between the twentieth and thirtieth years of your investment. That's fifty thousand dollars a year, which happens to be the amount you invested to begin with. That's the magic of compound interest. If you keep your money in an account without withdrawing it, you earn a rate of return on ever-larger amounts of money. In this case, no matter how much you invest, you're making it back every year for those ten years. Then you're making more after those ten years. You can see why it's intelligent to be an ROI sleuth. As an investor, your only goal is to make the most return consistently.

In fact, I'm such a nut over the ROI idea that I've even applied it to my college education. Imagine that college will cost $25,000 a year for four years of wonderful, expensive, private education. During those four years I'll be soaking up knowledge and I won't be earning a dime. Before I enter, I'm just a bumbling young fool. But when I graduate, I'm a college-educated bumbling young fool. I figure that the job I get with my degree, which happens to be in finance, will pay at least $60,000 a year. College will cost a grand total of $100,000 ($25,000 x 4). Let's say I spend $40,000 of that $60,000 from my first year on expenses and taxes. That means I still have $20,000 left over—a profit—from my earnings. Divide that $20,000 by $100,000 and you get a 20% return. So I've figured that my college education is giving me a 20% return on investment in the first year. By my definition that's a good return. College may still be expensive, but at least I'll be getting something back for my troubles.

Let's expand the idea of compound interest now. Take billionaires, for example. There are only about one hundred billionaires today. They take, on average, twenty years to gain their wealth. Many of them start with limited amounts of money. Sometimes it's a bit of their own mixed with just a few thousand from friends and family. Going from thousands to billions: that's quite a distance. As their wealth snowballs, they can use more to create more. Microsoft isn't an individual, but it's an amazing example of a company doing this. Microsoft makes much of the software used on your computer. As the company has made more money, they have invested in different ventures. Microsoft used to just make operating systems, software like Windows or its predecessor, DOS. In fact, they became rich with those products. But since then, they've used their increased purchasing power to buy more companies and invest in different products. So now Microsoft makes not only operating software but joysticks, mouses (or should I say mice), the most visited sites on the Internet, and much more. They've literally compounded their wealth. The stock price increased from less than $1 per share to $100 in fewer than fifteen years. You'll learn about stock prices later, but that should strike you as at least a *little* amazing now.

Compound interest works because of consistency—consistently getting a percentage return over time. Most people fail to understand compound interest because they are too close to one of the two extremes: either being a gambler or being totally scared of risk. Investing, whether in a company you own all or part of (a stock, which we'll discuss later, represents partial ownership), isn't gambling. Gambling is going to a casino and expecting to make a high-percentage return on your money very quickly. That's certainly possible at the roulette or craps table, yet casinos make billions of dollars a year. Las Vegas isn't shrinking—not, at least, when billion-dollar hotels sport million-dollar art collections. That's because you can't *consistently* win at craps or poker, even though you may have a big win once in a while. Compound interest isn't being right all of the time, either. Entrepreneurs, the people who take the initial risk

The Compound Interest Game

Let's play a game. You have two choices in this game. You can choose a flat payment of $10 million. Or I'll give you a penny, and I'll double it once a day for thirty days. Which would you prefer? I asked this question to a group of high school seniors, many of whom were going on to prestigious institutions like Yale and Stanford. At least half answered the flat payment. That, of course, is the wrong answer. (Why would I make this easy?) A penny doubled once a day for thirty days gives you nearly $11 million. As you can see, many intelligent people don't understand compound interest. Yet, that's the most important concept in wealth creation in the world.

to start their own companies, as well as the investors who fund them from the beginning, take large but wise risks.

I've never heard of anyone who took wise risks and was unsuccessful in life. Although they may have failed from time to time, they didn't get hurt too badly. Ultimately, the only way to never lose is to never play. If you play basketball, you (or your team) play to win. But the championship basketball team loses possession of the ball every three minutes. Failure is a part of the game. So in one respect, you play to win. But in another, basketball's a test of your resolve. It's a test of how well you can lose without being knocked out of the game completely. Young players, as well as young investors, fall victim to the idea that they'll never lose. Inevitably, when they do, they haven't prepared themselves and they can't deal with the game any more.

So compound interest works in the same respect. In fact, all investment, including investing time, energy, and resources into your own business, involves discipline. Great investors realize America is the home of capitalism, free enterprise with limited government restriction, and that it's possible to get rich in America. Most people are stuck with monotonous work because they are either looking for a big immediate payoff from their investing or they're looking for a way to make money without losing any of it. Winners fall in between these two extremes. Unfortunately, in times of prosperity, the gambling instinct takes over, and in times of depression the totally risk-averse side takes over. As we further discuss the specifics of investing, we'll see how it's possible to take advantage of both extremes for handsome profits.

As an investor, you're looking for that high rate of return. That means you're searching for the best **assets**. You may have heard of assets and **liabilities**. These are fancy finance terms that accountants flash around a lot. But they are really simple things.

The chart on top of page 10 is called a **balance sheet**. All companies produce a balance sheet. Unfortunately, they don't look this simple (and they have a lot more numbers). This is a simpler version of the balance sheet; it's a statement of assets and liabilities for an individual, not a corporation. At the top, it reads, "Assets: Anything that puts money in your pocket." I read this definition in a book called *Rich Dad, Poor Dad* by Robert Kiyosaki, a book which simplified the idea down to its essence. But what exactly do assets do? Look at stocks, for example. Stocks and bonds take your money and they make more of it. Like the

Assets	Liabilities
Anything that puts money into your pocket	Anything that takes money out of your pocket
Stocks, bonds, real estate, bank accounts & investments	Credit card debt, loans, IOUs
Royalties, patents, etc.	All expenses (cars, food, living)
Businesses that you don't work at	

bank account that gives you your money back plus some more, stocks and bonds give you a return over your initial investment. But liabilities just drain money from your pocket.

You may notice that in the table under "assets" I've included "businesses that you don't work at." How could these possibly exist? In the future, you should aim to create a successful business that can last without you. You may still draw a paycheck from this business, but you've done a good enough job that it can now run without you investing your time in it. This kind of self-sufficient business can be a really profitable asset.

The next chart is called an **income statement**. We'll relate the two charts in a second:

Income	Expenses
Money you get from anything	Money you have to spend and won't get back
Dividends on stocks and bonds, as well as profit from stocks and bonds	Payment for a new car
Payments from businesses	Restaurant bills

Notice a very important relationship: Assets produce income; liabilities subtract expenses. That means that your stock portfolio isn't any good if you waste your profits on a new car. It's fun to drive off the lot in a brand new automobile, but it isn't profitable. A new car, for instance, is immediately worth less than the purchase price after it's driven off the lot. A car payment is a liability because it requires money to be paid and it doesn't generate any income in return. On the other hand, your collector Pogs that you got tired of a few years ago still count as assets. They aren't really good assets, though, because they don't generate any income. And if you wanted to sell them, it would be very difficult to sell at a higher price than you bought them.

So here's the scoop on how to get rich: I call it the vicious circle of assets, although it's really quite pleasant. As you buy assets, they produce income. That income is used to buy more assets, and so on. Eventually you'll have enough money to waste on collector action figures or, as the case might be in twenty years, the collector Ferrari.

OK, you know some basic financial rules. Let's dive into investing.

Summary: In this chapter, we learned . . .
- It's okay to learn about money and use that knowledge to make money.
- Investing means taking a risk by putting your money into something that will give you your money back plus more money. Over time, that extra money can make you very rich.
- Assets put money in your pocket *without* any effort from you. Liabilities take money from your pocket. Assets produce income, which allows you to buy more assets or add to the size of your current ones (buy more stocks, for example).

Wet Feet on the Street

Before I first visited Wall Street, I had heard it was congested, full of bustling people. Whoever told me that was right and then some. Wall Street wasn't congested, it was packed—people waving their arms, people on telephones—people everywhere. But when I accepted the fact that every ten seconds somebody would bump me, I got around to the real fun: exploring things I had only read about. I could identify every building on the Street. I knew where the New York Stock Exchange was. When I went inside the Exchange, I knew the title of every character running around on the floor. I understood the responsibilities of the specialist and the floor trader, and I understood what every quote on the ticker meant. It all made sense, and I bubbled with excitement.

When you finish this chapter, you'll understand the terms and the feelings I speak of. That's because it's fun to understand something most people think is complex. A lot of people don't bother to invest because they can't understand all the information that's out there. They don't understand the key terms, and it's this first stumbling block that ends their adventure.

Remember that you don't have to know everything about stocks. However, you should be able to understand what people are talking about, and you should be able to communicate intelligently with them. Once you understand the terms, watching even the most advanced financial television show will be a breeze. Web sites and TV commentators use jargon more than anyone else, and you'll be able to understand their code after reading this chapter.

So let's begin in the beginning, and ask the fundamental question:

What is Wall Street?

Wall Street, or "the Street," is in the Financial District in New York City. However, "the Street" refers to the whole area, not *just* the street itself. What's so fascinating about Wall Street is that it's the center of investing and all investing-related services in the world. Wall Street shelters the **New York Stock Exchange (NYSE)**, the oldest and most prestigious of the stock exchanges. Several investment banking, management consulting, and brokerage firms also make their homes in Wall Street. You may recognize the names Merrill Lynch and Goldman Sachs, for example. Both are prominent investment banks and brokerages that are located on the Street. We'll talk about investment banking as it relates to stocks later, but suffice it to say that these firms earn *billions* every year.

Wall Street is the center of the universe when it comes to stocks. On the floor of the New York Stock Exchange, trillions of dollars change hands. While the system of transaction isn't complex, don't be fooled into thinking it's easy, either.

In a stock exchange, the stocks of individual companies are *traded*. In other words, people place buy and sell orders for a specific company, like IBM or Microsoft. We'll talk momentarily about the details of stocks, but let's talk about how the exchange works first.

In the New York Stock Exchange, **floor traders**, who work for brokerage houses, place these buy and sell orders for thousands of customers to a **specialist**, who trades, on average, six stocks. A specialist is just that, controlling the flow of buy and sell orders for a specific stock, like IBM. Brokerage houses are middlemen, connecting the buyer of the stock and the seller. If you enter an order to buy a stock, the broker will electronically send the order to a floor trader. If the order is large, the floor trader will negotiate with the specialist to get the best price. If the order is smaller, it's routed directly to what's called the specialist's book, a list of every buy and sell order the specialist has. Then the specialist fits all the buy and sell orders together, and hammers out any inconsistencies by trading the stock for his own account. He's the money manager, and the NYSE is filled with thousands of them. Every post you see with a computer has a specialist, making sure everything's running smoothly. The NYSE is organized chaos. On the one hand, there are thousands of order slips, indicating buy and sell orders, discarded on the floor (imagine being the janitor!). On the other hand, thousands of orders are placed, received, and executed efficiently every day. As Geoffrey Rush said in *Shakespeare in Love*, "Somehow, it will all work out."

Still, all this mess can get annoying. A few people got fed up with it, and they created the **NASDAQ** (National Association of Securities Dealers Advanced Quotation system). The NASDAQ is much more efficient, since everything is done on computer. It's a lot more pleasant to use. Things happen faster, and it's more precise. NASDAQ has no specialists. There is no central trading floor.

As a result, people are trading NASDAQ stocks more and more, and it's quickly becoming the most popular exchange. The NYSE has fallen out of favor. People think of it as a good old boy's club, with traders sipping martinis during lunch and profiting from their clients' näiveté. None of this is true, of course. At least most of it isn't. The exchange has changed a lot in two hundred years, but it's still messy and inadequate compared to the NASDAQ. And NASDAQ is the home of a lot of technology stocks, such as Microsoft, and Internet stocks, such as Yahoo!. With the growth of computers, technology has become one of the most popular investments. As a result, within just the last ten years NASDAQ has become a household name.

The NASDAQ and NYSE are stock exchanges, but each is part of the general idea known as the **stock market.** Have you ever heard your parents talk about "the market," as in, "The market's up today?" What are they talking about? When I first heard it, I though it was a reference to the prices at the supermarket. Yeah, yeah, it's hokey, but that's what I thought: "Market went up—damn supermarket now charges more for tomatoes than ever." Actually, they're talking about a **stock market index**, or a measurement of several stocks all squeezed into one number. This may sound confusing and complicated to compute, but it's easy, and you'll see the number enough to become familiar with it.

The three best known indices are the **Dow Jones Industrial Average** (DJIA); or Dow, the **NASDAQ Composite**; and the **Standard & Poor's 500** (S&P 500). The DJIA is by far the oldest. Dow Jones and Company started the index in the late 1890s to measure the market. The Dow Jones Company still exists, and so does the average. It measures thirty stocks on the New York Stock Exchange. Stocks are added and removed sometimes, but the thirty are always big names, like American Express and McDonald's. The Dow Jones company publishes *The Wall*

Street Journal, and the editors of the newspaper meet regularly to update which stocks are included in the index.

The NASDAQ composite is a composite index, meaning that it measures every stock on the NASDAQ and weighs each according to size. That means a large company like Microsoft makes up a bigger portion than a small biotechnology company. The same is true for the S&P 500, which are five hundred top companies ranked by Standard & Poor's, a prestigious stock market analysis firm. They're not always the biggest, but S&P considers them the best. And the big ones are always given a larger share of the pie than the smaller companies, like in the NASDAQ composite. S&P 500 companies can be on any exchange.

Once you understand what these indices are about, forget them. Learn to forget what the market does every day. You have no control over the Dow, the NASDAQ, or the S&P 500. You can't predict where they'll be in a week. You can't predict where they'll be tomorrow. Don't worry if the Dow surpasses 10,000, or if it surpasses 20,000—these are arbitrary numbers. Do, however, make certain that you invest wisely in good companies. Speculation, prediction, and worry over an index doesn't accomplish anything—intelligent investing does.

So what exactly are stocks?

We've talked a lot about the general markets, but you might be wondering: What exactly are stocks? You probably have a fuzzy idea of what they are. When I first started, I vaguely associated them with companies. I would hear someone say, "If you had bought one thousand shares of Wal-Mart twenty years ago, you would be worth several million dollars now." The *several million dollars* part caught my attention. I never understood what a "share" was, or where I could buy one. At first I thought you could walk into Wal-Mart and buy a few thousand shares just by asking a clerk.

In reality, **stocks,** also known as **equities,** are part ownership in a public company. Each slice of the company is called a **share**. Since companies are so large, they often have millions of shares available. That means several thousand people are considered shareholders, or part owners. Each share has a price. That's the number you hear about going up or down each day. The price that you hear about on the news is the price of just one share. But most people own more than one share. The pie is big enough to be controlled by many people, so a shareholder may have five hundred shares. If, for example, the price of each share is $10, this person has $5,000 worth of stock.

As a person who owns shares, or a **shareholder**, you get a few rights. Not many, but a few. You get what's called a **proxy vote**. That means you can vote on issues such as whether the company should increase the number of shares (yes, we'll talk about this later) or whom it should appoint to its board of directors. You receive one vote per share. People who own large numbers of shares have more votes than you, and thus they have more clout when the company asks the shareholders for a decision. It's clear that someone with big bucks and a large portion of the shares can vote himself onto the board of directors. The little investor doesn't have it great, but the proxy system isn't that bad. For one, it's easy to vote: all you have to do is fill out the form that your broker will send to your house. You check whether you abstain, accept, or reject the proposal(s). And you do get some say, no matter how small.

As I said earlier, trillions of dollars in orders flow through a stock exchange every day. Stock prices move up and down swiftly and for no reason. If stocks are going up, you'll hear people saying the market is in a **bullish** mode; if they're going down, it's in a **bearish** mode. People also use it to make intelligent-sounding predictions. It sounds coarse to say: "I think the stock's going up." Instead, bigwigs say, "I'm bullish on that stock for the next quarter." It's unnecessarily fancy, but use it to your advantage. Think of the stock market as a daily tug of war: Bulls in one direction, bears in the other. Bulls buying, bears selling. Whoever wins, wins. But everyone has to come back and fight tomorrow.

So you know the animals on Wall Street. How about something more substantial? Like, how do I find out how much my stock is worth? Who won the battle: the bulls or the bears? This changes every minute, and with the precision of computers you can check the price of a share every second. When you check the price, you're checking a **quote**. That's because the stock market is a real, live auction. If you've ever used the Internet site eBay, you've been part of an auction. At eBay, a seller puts an item up for sale and several people compete to buy the item. The same thing happens with stocks, with bidders trying to buy shares and sellers trying to get rid of them.

Like an auction, there are two prices, a **bid** and an **ask**. Let's say you want to buy a certain stock. You want to pay $20 for the stock. That's your bid. Well, the guy who owns the stock wants to sell his stock for the highest price possible for the highest profit. He'll sell the stock to you at $21. This is his offer, or "ask" price. Through an agreement, you decide to exchange the stock for $20.50. That's a fair compromise. This sort of thing happens every day between thousands of people and billions of shares. Usually, however, there are people waiting in line to buy at $20, and there are people in line to sell at $21. In fact, people are usually willing to buy at increments of $20, such as $20\frac{1}{16} or $20\frac{1}{8}, and are willing to sell at $20\frac{7}{8} or $20\frac{15}{16}. The price that the stock trades at is simply the price at which everyone is willing to compromise. In other words, the price of the stock in the example may be $20\frac{1}{2} or $20\frac{3}{4} or $20\frac{15}{16} or whatever the price is that the two market players agree on to exchange stock.

We call the difference between the bid and ask price the **spread**. In general, you'll find the spreads in the stock market to be very tiny. In fact, the NASDAQ has tiny spreads—usually $\frac{1}{16}$ of a dollar per share. This has given the NASDAQ a big boost over the years, since people who trade stocks like small spreads. Small spreads allow you to buy and sell your stock quickly without suffering.

Let's use the last example to demonstrate this. Assume you're a third person in the example. Joe wants to buy at $20 and Mary wants to sell for $21. You come in, and you want to buy. What price would you have to pay to buy? To buy immediately, before Joe and Mary agree to trade at $20.50 as they did earlier, you'd have to pay $21 to pick up the stock from Mary. So you buy, and then you decide quickly that you don't want the stock anymore and that you want to sell. To sell, you'd have to let Joe buy it at $20. You can't buy or sell the stock at $20.50, because you want to buy (or sell) the stock before they reach a compromise. By doing this, you'll lose a dollar in the process ($21 minus $20). When there are more people in the market, the spreads are smaller. In other words, some people may be ready to compromise by selling at $20\frac{1}{4} and buying at $20\frac{3}{4}. In real life, the spread is even smaller—$\frac{1}{16}$ or $\frac{1}{8}$ at most. The greater number of players means more people willing to compromise at certain prices.

Although the price is a key element of the stock, there are other issues. Most investors, unfortunately, *only* look at the price information from a stock quote, specifically an **extended quote**. An extended quote has all the vital information: how much the underlying business is worth, how much people in the market think it's worth, and how much profit it makes. I rarely check quotes, and you'll see why in later chapters. To be a well-informed investor, though, you should understand what's on the page. This quote will serve as a gateway to understanding all of the elements of a stock. Here's a sample of one such quote, similar in form to the quotes you can find on Yahoo!.

MICROSOFT CORPORATION (MSFT)

Last Trade Feb 19 * 147 3/4	Change +2 (1.37%)	Prev Cls 145 3/4	Volume 18,271,400	Div Date Feb 1998
Day's Range 145 3/4 – 149 1/4	Bid 147 10/16	Ask 147 11/16	Avg Volume 15,243,318	Ex-Div Feb 1998
52 Week Range 78 7/8 – 175 15/16	Earn/Shr 2.35	P/E 62.02	Mkt. Cap 372.8 B	Div/Shar & Yield N/A

This quote is from Microsoft Corporation, and it's a quote from the end of the day. The "MSFT" by the name of the company is the **ticker symbol**. The ticker is an important sequence of letters. It's your introduction to the stock. Any time you are on the Internet and you are asked to enter the ticker symbol, you'll need to know this sequence of letters. For new investors, you'll be acquainted with only a few stocks, and the tickers will be easy to memorize. Most Internet services that have quotes offer you an opportunity to look up a company to find its symbol. Once you know that, you can go explore the whole quote.

The first box in the table above is simple: the date (February 19) and the price per share. The next box to the right includes the change from the close of the previous day (up two dollars per share, or **points**,) and what percentage that is of the total price. Do you see that $2 is 1.37% of $145? In other words, $2 divided by $145 equals .0137, or 1.37%. It's important to note that percentage movements are *far* more important than total price movements. For example, the Dow Industrial Average may fall 137 points in one day. However, if the Dow's price is at 10,000, this is a 1.37% move, exactly the same thing as if Microsoft falls only $2 per share.

Next, we see that the previous close is yesterday's close. The **volume** is the number of shares traded that day. Near holidays and other off times, the volume "dries up." It falls to, oh, only a few hundred million shares on the NYSE. Other times, volume skyrockets, especially when a big piece of news comes out about a major company.

Next, a company can choose to pay out a portion of its profits to the investor as what's called a **dividend**. If it doesn't, it can keep its earnings. Why would a company pay out earnings if it could keep them? Tradition, in part. Large, well-established companies have been paying out dividends for years. Also, investors in the 1940s and 1950s tended to buy stocks with higher dividends. Tradition is changing, however. Today, more and more people are ignoring dividends. They'd rather see the company keep its earnings and plow them back into building the business.

A dividend is an actual check in the mail. While it may seem weird that a company pays out its earnings to the average Joe Investor, the idea of a dividend makes one thing clear: We are part owners in the company, and we get our share of profits. In our example, Microsoft chose not to pay out any earnings.

To me, dividends are very cool. They make me *feel* like a part owner. If a company doesn't pay out any dividends, I don't feel like I actually "own" the company. I still do, because what they don't pay out in dividends they're using themselves. But it's always fun to get a check in the mail, no matter how small. Save that money and put it back into your investments.

The **ex-dividend** date is when you need to have owned the stock before you can receive the dividend. That means you needed to buy this stock by February to receive the dividend (if they paid one out). Some companies are more restrictive—they make you purchase the stock months before the dividend is paid. Otherwise, people would buy stock just before the dividend was announced and then sell quickly after they got their check.

Next, the **day's range** is the total price movement during any day. Notice that Microsoft moves four points between the high and low price of the day. Some Internet stocks move as much as twenty points. The next two cells are the bid and the ask. We've already discussed the bid and the ask, but note how minor the price difference is—a sixteenth of a dollar. That's called a "teeny," because it's so small. It's also an example of how **liquid** the NASDAQ is. Liquid means that there's a lot of interest and enough stock to fill it. Microsoft, for example, is huge. It trades about 18,000,000 shares on an average day. And it has over two billion shares available! The company's worth on the market, also called the **market capitalization** or **market cap**, is $372 billion. The market cap is a fancy term for a simple calculation: It's the number of shares the company has multiplied by the price per share.

Our next topic, the **earnings per share** (Earn/shr), is worth keeping an eye out for. You'll find people make the biggest deal about this number. The earnings are the profits. Remember what profits are: The total amount of money you make minus the costs. If a company makes a million dollars, and it has a million shares, it's made one dollar per share in earnings.

Earnings per share are reported four times during a company's **fiscal year**. Companies can begin their fiscal year at different times, but the fiscal year is still twelve months long. For example, Microsoft's fiscal year begins July 1 and ends June 30. In Microsoft's case, since it begins its fiscal year in July, it would report first quarter earnings, also known as Q1 (second quarter earnings are known as Q2, etc.) in October.

The next important figure is the **price-to-earnings ratio**. You'll hear a lot about this on television and in other sources. Sometimes it's called the "valuation" or the "PE." If the price of the stock is $147 ¾ and the company made $2.35-per-share, the price-to-earnings is $147 ¾ ÷ $2.35, or 62, which you can see on the table. As the price of the stock gets higher, the P/E ratio will climb. People generally feel that stocks with high P/E ratios are already highly valued compared to their earnings and don't have much higher to go. Generally, this is true, but there are a few exceptions. At the time of this writing, stocks of companies that are on the Internet—Yahoo!, Amazon.com, eBay—have very high prices and very low earnings. In fact, many of the companies are losing money. As a result, a lot of people are worried about the P/E. They think it's far too high, and the stocks are in for a fall. However, the earnings are just one variable that affects the decision of somebody who wants to buy the stock. Another is the expectation of the future: If Joe thinks the stock is going to jump twenty points next month because it jumped twenty points last month, he'll buy regardless of whether the P/E is too high or no earnings exist.

Before we move into more about stocks, note that a quote is just a quick overview of a company. All of the information is available on the Internet, and there are some sites that specialize in distributing financial information. Later, we'll use them (and other cool sites) to find out all about a company.

Summary: In this chapter, we learned . . .
- How Wall Street manages all the trillions of dollars that change hands every day. We talked about the New York Stock Exchange, the biggest on Wall Street, as well as the up-and-coming NASDAQ.
- We talked about the major stock market indices: The Dow and the S&P 500. While we don't check them every day, we know that they represent the movements of thirty different stocks for the Dow and five hundred for the S&P index.
- The major elements of a stock quote. The price changes every day, going up or down. Other parts of the "extended quote" include the P/E ratio, the earnings per share, and dividends. Review these if you forgot what they mean.

3

Life Cycle of *Stockus Americanus*

Now that we've hacked that stock quote to death, let's talk about some things you could see happen to your stock. You shouldn't be surprised, for example, if you receive a check in the mail, discover that the price of your shares has split in half, or find that your stock has a new name. All these things happen to the most prestigious of stocks, and you'll find out all about them in our life-cycle view of stocks.

A stock is born through an **Initial Public Offering (IPO)**. The difficulties in getting a company to the stock market are tremendous. By virtue of a good stock market, head managers in companies can become very rich as the price of the stock that they own increases. The company in general can raise a lot of money by going public, and then they can pour that money back into the company. After the company's management team, the **investment banks** are the most key players in the IPO.

Before we continue, let's talk about investment banks, or I-banks as they're often called. I briefly mentioned that they were located on Wall Street, but we haven't talked about them since. Wall Street and the area surrounding it is home to large financial firms. Almost magically, many companies on Wall Street record billions of profit yearly. Very few people know what goes on inside these firms. Generally, the firms are divided into two divisions: Sales and Trading and Investment Banking. New employees usually begin as analysts in one of the divisions and eventually work their way up. We'll focus on I-banking now, but we'll talk about trading later. Investment bankers are the people who act as agents and counsel for their clients, aiding them in mergers, acquisitions, and new ventures. The real truth is that investment banks do give advice and help in the transaction, but they get a large (perhaps overly large) chunk of money for it.

For example, in our case, let's assume you run a company that's been around for five years. The company has grown a lot, but you're curious about what an IPO can do for you. You hire an investment bank, and they do their best to raise money for you. A required amount has to be raised to be listed on the stock market. This money is called **financing**, and it can come from a variety of sources. The investment bank has a hefty Rolodex chock-full of names and numbers of wealthy people and companies. In exchange for investing in the company, these people or companies receive **blocks**, or portions, of stock. For example, if I invest $1 million in this company, I'm allotted 10,000 shares even before the stock goes on the market. There's some uncertainty in that. If the price of the stock goes up when the company finally hits the market, I make a lot of money. If the stock market in general isn't that good, then I'm not going to fare well.

One type of organization that specializes in this type of investment is a venture capital company. **Venture capitalists** invest money in companies in their early stages. VCs, as they're called, take many risks. The risk of complete failure is much greater for a small start-up than it is for an established company. However, with those risks comes the potential for substantial rewards. If the companies become successful, those stakes can be worth millions. For example, in 1998, $5 billion poured into San Francisco's Silicon Valley, the home to many technology companies. With so much success in this industry, venture capitalists flock to the Valley, hoping to invest in the next Microsoft or Intel. Even though there's money at stake, the relationship between a venture capitalist and a start-up is a healthy one. The venture capitalist wants the company to succeed and make money, so they provide them with help in everything from setting up their offices to getting to the IPO.

After the company heads to the market, a number of things can happen. The company can flounder. It can become so unpopular, in fact, that there is too small of a bid price (the price somebody's willing to pay to buy the stock) and the stock will become **delisted**. Poof, gone. Or a stock could do excellently. Everybody wants it. It's so popular that it goes to $250 per share. So what does the company do? They split it. They double (or triple, or quadruple) the number of shares and split the price in two (or three, or four). This is called a **stock split**.

For example, OFC, Our Favorite Company, wants to split its stock. They have ten million shares and the price per share is $100. So they split the stock: Increase the number of shares to twenty million and split the price to $50 per share. Notice that the market capitalization—the number of shares multiplied by the price—remains the same: $1 billion. Companies split the stock so the shares look more attractive at a lower price per share. Two hundred dollars per share may leave a bitter taste in your mouth, but $50 looks better. It's a hackneyed marketing gimmick that almost every company uses. Most companies, however, do well by splitting their stock. It's sort of like a baby before it's born: Its cells keep dividing to let it grow.

To understand how stock splits can be effective is to understand Microsoft and its founder, William H. Gates, III. Ever heard of Bill Gates? He's the richest man in the world. You may have heard that he's made a million dollars a minute over the past ten years, or some other spin on that story. Well, he doesn't have the highest-income job in the world. He's no high-priced lawyer. His money is the result of owning an excellent stock. He owns a large portion (over sixty billion dollars worth, to be exact) of Microsoft stock because he's the founder of the company. He owned a large piece of the company when it first **went public,** meaning that it went onto the stock market through an IPO.

Since then, Microsoft has split numerous times. Each time it splits, the stock looks more attractive to investors, and they keep buying. It's deceptive: Microsoft is worth close to $400 billion on the market, meaning it's the most valuable stock in history. But its per-share price is close to $150, not even close to the highest-priced stock on the market (which is, for trivia's sake, Berkshire Hathaway—an excellent company that never split its stock and is worth around $70,000 per share).

Because of pure greed, many large companies will want to grow larger. Of course, all companies want to expand, but many don't have the resources to make major **acquisitions**. An acquisition occurs when one company purchases another. By doing so, they pay a certain number of dollars and they get, in return, all the company's assets and liabilities. In other words, they get control of the company's money machine. The terms "merger" and "acquisition" are often used interchangeably, but **mergers** are when one company buys another of a similar size. To do so, often the buyer will have to borrow a lot of money. Regardless, it isn't important to worry about mergers and acquisitions that much. With a basic understanding that companies can expand and contract (by buying or selling off divisions), you shouldn't have to worry when you hear that your company has been acquired or is acquiring.

Finally, in the life cycle of a stock, companies can choose to **spin off** profitable operations. A spin-off is a separate company with a separate stock. That doesn't seem natural—that a good company would want to get rid of a profitable part of itself. Well, it's a trick. It's not shady, but it's a trick, like a stock split. CBS Corporation, for example, decided to spin off their radio division. Their radio division is actually profitable, so they raised money with an IPO for the division, called Infinity Broadcasting Corp. (this actually happened, I'm not making the name up). They get some of that money to play with, and they also keep a chunk of shares, which makes them the biggest owner of the new company. CBS has made a wise choice. Study after study shows that spin-offs do better than the average stock. CBS has a good chance of making money in both the IPO and in the future, holding the stock.

In general, American businesses are a great place to put your money. Stocks in American companies are the place to be. At one time, it was popular to invest in companies around the world. In fact, it still is considered somewhat exotic to put money in other countries. People thought that Russia, Japan, and smaller Asian countries were excellent places to invest. All three markets crashed. That isn't investor stupidity, it's investor greed. These so-called **emerging markets** offer potentially great rewards, but there are substantial risks. There's the risk of rebellion overturning the government. There's the risk that the government may take action to restrict trade, laws that would be illegal in the United States. And even if these risks don't emerge, there's the risk that the economy may fail all by itself. Remember, America is the best and safest place to invest. There are plenty of valuable companies here.

With companies that can safely earn money year after year, it's far easier to take advantage of compound interest. If you remember our discussion in Chapter 1, you remember that compound interest *really* starts working in the later years. Here's a rule that should make sense of it all: Divide 72 by the percentage return you get on stock to determine the amount of time that your money takes to double. Let's say you make a return of 11% a year. You invest $1000 in the market. It takes a year to make $110 on that $1000. You say to yourself, "I work at a store in the mall and I make that kind of money in one week. Don't tell me people are getting rich doing that." But figure that the money will double, by the rule of 72, about every six and a half years (72 ÷11 equals about 6 ½), and in thirty years you could have $32,000.

And that's with only 11% a year. I'll show you how you can potentially make 20%, 30%, or more in the market. A disciplined investor starting in his early twenties and investing only $2000 a year could be worth over $6 million in forty years while making only 15% a year in the market! And that $6 million could produce up to $600,000 a year in retirement income. Now we're talking. You can probably shell out $2,000 (or more) every year with six million on your mind. Forty years sounds like a lot, but if you save more than $2,000 a year, you can definitely keep more faster.

The Rule of 72
No, it's not the mystical meaning of life. It's actually easy math. To find out how long it takes for a stock to double, divide 72 by your return or investment.
Let's say you can get 6% a year for the next ten years. Your investment will double in (Albert Einstein here I come) twelve years (72/6=12). Magic, I think not.

Unfortunately, you don't get to keep everything that you make. There's something called the **capital gains tax**, which takes a maximum of 20% of your profits that you've owned for more than a year. We'll talk about how this tax affects our strategy later. Don't worry, it won't hurt your nest egg too badly.

Even with the drawback of taxes, stocks are the finest investment around. In fact, the approach that we'll follow—a long-term, business-oriented approach—keeps stocks for years without selling. Because the tax only applies if you sell, this approach minimizes the affect of the tax.

All right, you know the drill about stocks. You can impress your friends with your business wisdom. Unfortunately, however, you can't just go to the exchange and ask for a few shares. You'll need a broker to help you make your first investments.

Summary: In this chapter, we learned . . .
- The life cycle of an American stock from its beginning as an IPO to a merger to a spin-off or delisting.

4

Baby Steps—The Brokerage Account

You've probably heard the horror stories about stock brokers. They call you during dinner and try to sell you on the next hot stock. They call you at 9 A.M. and tell you that you need to restructure your portfolio, buying and selling stocks in a transaction that would make them tons of cash. Well, the Internet has changed everything.

For the young investor, the Internet has made investing easier and far less expensive. And one of the most important parts of Internet investing is the brokerage account. When you're taking your baby steps into the stock market, the first step is this account. You're giving a large (it's all relative) amount of money to a company that will do the grunt work of investing for you. You'll pick the stocks, how much to buy, and when to buy. They do all the paperwork, they have the people on the exchange floors, and they actually buy the stock. It costs them a lot of money for the privilege of trading on the floor, and the brokerage house used to charge a lot of money to give you the privilege of buying and selling stocks. High commissions made people think that only the wealthy elite could dabble in stocks.

Things have changed. They've actually changed twice. In the mid-1970s, the government ended regulation of the **commission**. That's the price you have to pay a broker to buy or sell a stock for you. Usually it's a fixed price. At one point, the government forced brokerage companies to charge a certain minimum commission. Once that government power was removed, the flood gates opened. Brokerage houses everywhere offered cheap commissions. One of the first and certainly the most famous of these "discount brokerages" was Charles Schwab, a company that rapidly developed around low prices and good service.

What looked like a discount then looks like a rip-off today. Schwab could get away with charging $100 commissions. That meant that if you tried to buy or sell a stock, you'd have to pay $100 to buy and $100 to sell. That's awfully expensive, and on top of it you had to give a percentage of your profits to the government.

Besides high commissions, offline brokers are famous for their notoriously pushy stock brokers. Stock brokers make a lot of money on their commissions, and so they like people to buy and sell a lot. They're also world-famous for the cold call, in which they call you up without any notice (it always seems like they call during dinner, too) and try to sell the "hot new stock." Of course, people are suckered into buying the stock because they think their broker is giving them an in on a special investment. The truth is, in fact, that stock brokers have to sell a certain number of these stocks anyway, and most of them are dogs with fleas. In fact, most human brokers have a VIP list of people with lots of money that they do actually give the potentially profitable public offerings to. That's because these people benefit *them* in an important way— their pocket—with the high commissions they can charge. Of course, most young people that I know aren't wealthy and don't have these special privileges. As a result, we're forced to rethink our strategy.

Internet Brokers: Welcome to the New World

I'm ruthless when it comes to Internet brokers. Most of them do the same thing, so why pay more for the same product? You shouldn't. Of course, there are several caveats. Some brokers aren't very reputable. You should be able to contact the broker via phone or regular mail. Now, you may ask, how can I easily distinguish the thieves from the good guys? A simple litmus test is where they advertise. If you see a broker advertised on television, a popular business magazine like *Fortune*, or a popular Web site like Yahoo!, they probably are reputable. That doesn't mean that just because you can see them they're good. It just means that they have the cash to advertise, and they're taking too great a risk of lawsuit by advertising falsely on television.

Overall, though, the Internet is a blessing. In a perfect world, everyone would use the Internet to buy things. Items are cheaper on the Internet. Some items are of better quality. But people are still anchored to their old relationships with stock brokers. They refuse to believe the truth, which is that brokers are glorified salespeople. Be truthful with yourself. Invest on the Internet.

The Internet is the most important change to the industry since the discount brokerage. Internet users can bypass these pesky brokers and do their own investing, without anyone hassling them. Since Internet brokerages don't have to pay for brick-and-mortar offices or salespeople, they can charge lower commissions. Today, it's foolish to use anything *but* an Internet broker. Human brokers are a dying breed, as they should be. Today it pays to gather the knowledge yourself, and then trade on your own. When you look for a broker, you should be interested only in a few things. A Liebowitz Law that you should always follow is:

Consider (1) price and (2) customer service as the most important keys when choosing a brokerage.

That eliminates brokerage houses that aren't on the Internet. And the ones that are on-line are trying to justify higher commissions. A lot of the old firms charge $60 or $80 to make a trade via their Internet service. Supposedly, that's merited by a higher quality of service. Rubbish. No matter how much you pay to make a trade, you'll still be talking to a broker—a trained sales professional. You aren't talking to the guy who manages a successful fund, or the investor whose expertise has helped him become very rich. You're talking to a guy who sells stocks for a living. Some people sell cars, he sells stocks. The only reason you would want to talk to a human being is if you had some specific criteria regarding when to buy your stock, such as if it hit a certain number. However, your goal is to become a young investor, not a young trader. Make good decisions and don't worry about the small stuff—like whether the stock goes up or down each day or the *exact, to-the-fraction* price you pay for it. Since you're not going to do this, you won't need an expensive broker.

What's the cheapest price you can pay for a commission? Five dollars. I've seen that price at Brown & Co. (www.brownco.com), but to join you must have a certain number of years of experience in the markets as well as $10,000 to invest. Five or ten years from now, that may be penny change, but now it may be too much. Ameritrade offers $8 trades, and all Datek trades cost $10. Schwab and Merrill Lynch both charge about $30 per trade. And I imagine that many other firms will begin lowering their costs and switching to on-line service.

Since the price differences aren't that substantial, and you won't be doing many trades, use the service you feel comfortable with. I've seen all the services described here, and while the low commissions are an important enough reason to stick with on-line brokerages, they aren't important enough to sacrifice customer service. The two most important elements of choosing a broker are low commissions and comfort. If you're not comfortable, it definitely can and should affect your choice. For example, Ameritrade forced me to wait half an hour on the phone before I could speak to anyone about reactivating my account, after an error that wasn't my fault. On the flip side, I've found no problems with Ameritrade's real service—executing trades. And Ameritrade has a low account limit—as low as $500—which is attractive for the new investor.

Datek is the best service for the active trader. With few exceptions, traders who buy and sell a lot drive themselves into the ground and pay out thousands of dollars in commissions and taxes. All brokerages love commissions, and so they encourage people to trade actively. Although they don't have your best interests at heart, they can't force you to trade more than you want to. Datek offers free real-time updating of quotes. For you, that's a bit extravagant. Even if you had an old *Wall Street Journal* to find quotes, you'd still fare pretty well using long-term methods. Most services offer **delayed quotes,** quotes that are twenty minutes delayed from the exchange, which are suitable for your purposes. If your investment scope is many years, twenty minutes doesn't mean much. But if you're a rapid trader, a second means as much as years mean to me. This aside, Datek offers fast trading, and every order is set at $10, even limit orders, which most brokerage houses charge more for. E-Trade offers $15 trades and underwhelming service. They've had several service outages where no trades could be executed.

If you're gung-ho about service, go with Charles Schwab. Time after time, they receive good reports from people. They're the most successful on-line brokerage, even though they weren't the first. And they charge more than most. If price was the only issue, people wouldn't flock to them. But price isn't the only issue, and their customer service is second to none.

Of course, there are others out there, and I encourage you to do your own research. The material in this book is inevitably dated. At any time, a broker could lower their commissions or improve their service. What won't change is the Internet: I'm convinced it's the only way to trade cheaply and effectively.

Once you make the choice, how does it work from there? You call up the broker or go to their Web site, and you can print out an application. You have to sign this and send it in with a check. Once you have an account with a number and a password, you can begin to invest. As a side note, the account you'll have is called a **custodial account**. You may find that it's listed as a UGMA account, a Uniform Gifts to Minors Act account. You have free reign in it, but it's under your parent's name. That means that you can't do any fancy, risky stuff like sell short or trade options (which you shouldn't be doing anyway).

When you first log on to this account, all the choices may be confusing. Not only can you buy and sell, you can sell short and buy to cover, use a limit or a stop order, or even a stop limit order. Here are a few of the common orders explained. Even if you never use some of them, you should be privy to what people are talking about when they refer to them. These may be confusing at first, but that's okay, you'll mostly be dealing with the first.

• **Market Order:** Enter the number of shares you want to buy. Your order will go through quickly because you will always be buying on the ask (remember the bid/ask spread?) and selling on the bid. For example, if the bid was 50 and the ask was 50 ½, that means there's a seller at 50 ½ and a buyer at 50. If you had a market order to buy, you'd quickly be matched with the seller, paying $50 ½ per share for your shares. If you wanted to sell, you'd quickly be matched with the buyer at $50 per share for your shares.

• **Limit Order:** The limit order means that you buy a stock at a certain price. The price is always lower than the current price. An example of a limit order would be an order to buy a stock at $64 ½ when the stock was at $64 ¾. People ask me: Why can't I enter a limit order so I buy when the stock goes up? If you were to do that, you'd be the only fool who paid, say, $65 a share for a stock when the price is $60. You'd pay $65, and the price would go back to $60. Don't do that!

• **Stop Loss Order:** The stop order allows you to sell a stock at market price when it hits a certain price. That price is lower than the current price, allowing you to cut your losses. For example, if you have a stop loss at $60 on a stock you buy at $65, once the price hits $60 the stock will automatically be sold at the bid price. Cutting your losses is extremely valuable in short-term trading. Don't get too excited by this type of order, though. It's not good to sell your stock hastily after a small dip in the price. In fact, by doing so, you'll minimize your chances of a really good long-term gain. You'll discover that long-term investors don't need stop losses. They minimize risk by investing intelligently.

• **Selling Short and Buying to Cover:** Reverse capitalism at its finest. The mantra of stock investing is "buy low, sell high." Selling short reverses that: "Sell high, buy low." When you enter an order to sell short, you're borrowing the shares and then selling them. You haven't spent any of your own money. What you hope is that the stock will go down, and then you want to "cover your short." That means you use the cash in your account to buy back the stock at a lower price. The difference is your profit.

Here's an example. You decide ABC stock is going to fall. The current price is $90. You sell one hundred shares short. That means you borrow the one hundred shares, and then sell them (you don't have to arrange the borrowing, the order does it automatically). Now you have $9,000 cash in your account, but you *have* to buy the shares back. If the stock falls to $85, you can purchase your one hundred shares, or buy to cover, at $85, or for a total of $8500. The difference—$500—is yours to keep. On the other hand, if the stock price rises to $95, you'll have to buy back your one hundred shares for $95, meaning you'd pay $9500. If you initially had $9,000 in your account, you'd have a negative balance, which definitely *isn't* a good thing. Conceivably, the stock can go up forever. If the stock went to $300, you'd have to pay back $300,000. Not exactly a wise bet.

Short selling has received a bad name in recent years, largely because of the booming stock market. People also don't like the idea of betting that something will fail—it feels un-American. There's some truth in that, especially because selling short is nerve-wracking. You have to watch the price constantly and make sure the stock isn't turning against you by going up. You don't have the confidence of buying the shares of an excellent company. Companies do fail, however. *A lot* of companies fail. Still, steer clear of selling short, unless you want to devote hours to learning to trade.

Once you enter an order, the broker routes it through the computer system to the floor of the exchange. For the NYSE, the order is put into the specialist's order book. The NASDAQ is more computerized. All the orders are fed directly into a computer system which displays all of the orders. You'll receive a confirmation. File it away somewhere safe; it's necessary for reporting your taxes. All brokerage houses report trades to the IRS, so if you don't report them also you'll be in trouble. However, the investment strategies in this book involve a minimum amount of reporting because you'll be doing a minimum amount of selling. You'll be charged a tax, which can be a maximum of 20% of your profits, only when you sell (you get charged more if you hold the stock less time). This will also keep your parents off your neck, since you'll be filing only a few trades on their tax return!

The Internet can't eliminate stock brokers, but it makes them a lot cheaper. Live with stock brokers, don't live with high prices. If your parents try to convince you that it's best to go with a human broker, they're scared. People don't like to make a go at things without any help, even when the help isn't worth the price.

Summary: In this chapter, we learned . . .
- In their long history, brokerage firms have overcharged customers considerably. Discount brokerages changed that, and now Internet brokerages are lowering prices even more.
- Shop around on the Net for low prices and good service. Low prices should come first, but the on-line brokerage sites shouldn't be complex to use or difficult to contact. Customer service can be key.
- The most common type of order is the market order, which is instantly executed. A limit order sets a specific price to buy or sell a stock, and a stop order is a market order to sell when a certain price is hit, thereby quickly stopping a further loss.

5

Sources of Information

I once thought CNBC was the greatest channel in the world.

I quickly learned that it isn't. CNBC offers nonstop financial news before, during, and after market hours. Only after 7:00 P.M. do they stop talking about the stock market. Here's what happens on the channel: The newsperson talks about how well or poorly the market did during the day, and then he or she invites their guest to speak about the market. It's Mr. Genius at the Prudent Bear Fund. Of course, he says, "It's amazing. This market is totally overpriced! I foresee the market dropping *40%* in the next six months." He says this with complete sincerity, as if he knew that mankind was doomed and he could do nothing about it.

Next, the CNBC anchor thanks him and they bring a new guest on the air. He works for some prominent firm on Wall Street as well, and he says, "I think the market's way undervalued, and it's going to go as high as such-and-such number by the end of the year." So here we have two smart people with several advanced degrees between them who have looked at the same information and have come up with two totally different predictions for the future.

So how do you deal with this? First of all, you have to totally disregard what everybody says. Have no respect for authority (that doesn't mean to disrespect it, though!). The idea that "experts" exist in finance is silly. The idea that they can tell the future is plain stupid. However, the media has conditioned us to believe that if someone went to Harvard and works at a prestigious firm, he must be able to tell the future.

For example, if a stock analyst makes a prediction and she's right, everybody thinks, "Wow, she must know what she's talking about. Her reasons sound pretty intelligent." Take the example of Abby Joseph

Cohen. She works for Goldman Sachs, and she has a nice office. She's a managing director at the firm, the highest position, and she's articulate and intelligent. For years, she has been saying the market is going to go up. But she's not always right about the number. She said the Dow Industrial Average would be at 10,000 almost a year before it hit that number. Regardless, people listen to her every word, thinking she's some kind of oracle who can see the future.

People are wrong. And when the market starts heading south, everybody will say, "Oh, Mr. Genius from the Prudent Bear Fund seems to know where the market's going," even though he was dead wrong when the market was heading up.

Thus, another Liebowitz Law is as follows:

Know the news, not what people think of it.

Besides the experts, the news media interprets the news. They're supposed to be an unbiased source, but we hear their opinion every day. Let's look at an example. Disney comes out with some bad news. Their parks aren't making a lot of money. The stock goes up. Yes, that's right: The stock goes up. The commentator or news report will say, "Disney announced today that park revenues have gone down. Investors shrugged off the news as the stock gained half a point." This is incorrect. Investors never "shrug off" bad news. There are a lot of smart people on Wall Street, and rumors get started very quickly. People knew the park revenues were hurting, so in the past few days the stock probably fell in price. When the news finally came out, the smart people started buying back their stock. An old adage says, "Buy on the rumor, sell on the fact." The smart money does just the opposite for bad news. They sell on the rumor, buy on the fact.

With so many different players, it's impossible to predict the market from day to day. But people can't embrace mystery. They need everything explained for them, and the news people fulfill this need by interpreting the news for them. Over time, the markets have followed an upward path. Quality stocks go up and poor ones go down. But focusing on a specific day and trying to explain the price action for that day is useless. Instead, focus on the larger picture—the business behind the stock. Let daily price movements be a mystery. You don't have to know everything.

Watching the Tube

Watching television to get your news isn't—in and of itself—bad. However, when I talk to people who watch the television business shows, I find them overly preoccupied with being up to the moment about news. While being interested is good, being worried isn't. Finance programs on television inspire frenzy and fear. On top of that, what you see on television is still the media's interpretation of the news. The news has passed through someone else's lens.

The first problem is that all the shows, in general, make a priority of having the presidents or Chief Executive Officers (CEOs) of companies on television. Just the other day, I saw Jeff Bezos, CEO of Amazon.com, on a prominent television show. As a note, remember that Internet companies did wonderfully in the stock market in 1999. Most of them didn't make a dime in profit, but their stock prices went through the roof. Anyway, the host of the show asked a good question: "How do you plan to make a profit?" And Bezos responded in some management mumbo-jumbo, repeating the phrase "customer-centric" several times. It may be good to be interested in your customers, but businesses aren't charities; profits are just as important. Of course, he had no idea how he was going to make a profit, but he was riding high on the stock price, which made him a billionaire nearly overnight.

I don't dislike Bezos. He seems amiable enough. But he's hyping his company. Hype is useless. The other day I read a story about an accounting company that had taken a full-page ad in a newspaper. They didn't fill the page with adjectives promoting their "excellent" services or "meticulous" standards. Instead, they gave proof. They told stories of happy clients, and they actually referred to their competitors as "quality companies." And guess what? Their company soared. Job applicants sought work there even though they never had heard of the company before. Potential clients called in droves. Salespeople, like Bezos, send one message across: "I want to sell you a product." For me, that doesn't cut it.

Newspapers: Reading the Fine Print

Newspapers are less fun than television. Television is a delightful mix of sound and story. Even most of the anchors and newsreaders are attractive and enjoyable to watch. But the newspaper is different. It magically appears at your doorstep every morning, and there isn't anybody to read it except you. Most teenagers find it tough to read a newspaper. I did when I started. "Who cares about all this junk?" I would say.

Eventually, however, I picked up a different newspaper—*Investor's Business Daily*. Now I suggest to everyone I meet who wants to learn about the stock market and business in general to read this newspaper or *The Wall Street Journal*. These newspapers offer so much more than your regular morning paper. Most of the information relates to business, so you learn about the economics of different companies. *Investor's Business Daily* has sections on specific industries, so every week I learn about different industries from clothing to gambling.

Now that you're a little smarter about the stock market, reading the financial newspaper will be great fun. Sometimes I bring the financial paper to public places, and people make fun of me. They laugh and point like I'm a zoo animal—"Oh, look, he's interested in investing." That's because business newspapers have a bad reputation. Very few "normal" people read them; they're mostly read by old, wealthy people. People imagine some millionaire reading *The Wall Street Journal* on his yacht or private plane. In the movie *The Thomas Crown Affair*, Pierce Brosnan's wealthy character is not reading just any paper, he's reading *The Wall Street Journal*.

What makes these papers seem so exclusive is the language. By now you know most of this jargon, and I've included a lot more in the glossary at the back of this book. For example, when a company decides they're going to go onto the stock market, the headline isn't JOE SCHMO'S GROCERY STORE TO GO ONTO THE STOCK MARKET. It's MORGAN STANLEY UNDERWRITES NEW JOE SCHMO IPO. In simpler terms, Morgan Stanley, a company that helps startups go public, is helping Joe Schmo put his company on the stock market through an IPO, an Initial Public Offering. We've talked about this already, but to refresh your memory: The IPO is the process of going public and listing your stock in a stock market. The newspaper makes it hard to understand, so a lot of people are scared of investing. I bet the number-one reason people don't invest as much as they should is that they open one of these papers. They're gung-ho to learn about investing, but once they open the paper, they feel like they're reading another language. If I wanted to learn Chinese, I wouldn't start by opening a Chinese newspaper—I'd be completely lost! So you have to adapt. Once you learn the financial jargon—and it's very easy—you'll be able to read the paper backwards and forwards like a pro.

If you really want to get into a specific paper, borrow the guide to the paper from the library. Usually business papers have a reader's guide that comes with the subscription. The guide is available at the library, or the guide may be in the paper itself, somewhere on the financial pages. Why is a guide necessary? Newspapers muck up even simple things, like stock quotes. Take a look at this:

Mcrsft 85½ +1 84½234000s

This is a quote from a large local paper. When I first looked at that in the paper, it made no sense to me. I had been investing for some time, but I'd never bothered to go to a newspaper for a stock quote. For some reason, the newspapers don't use the common "ticker symbol," which is the universal symbol for the stock. In this example we have a quote from some stock. It looks a lot like Microsoft. However, Microsoft's universal symbol is MSFT. I'm not too smart, so it took me some time to figure that this *was* Microsoft's name, with the vowels removed. And I had to page through an alphabetical list of several hundred stocks with the vowels in their names removed before I found this one.

What does it all mean? If you can read the fine print, with all the numbers crunched together, the "85½" is the last price, the "+1" is how much higher (or lower) it was than yesterday, and the "84½" is the previous close. The "234000" is the volume of the stock with the last two zeros removed, so the real number was 23,400,000. Somehow, the paper figures that removing the last two zeros saves a lot of newsprint. The "s" is a code meaning that the stock has already split. Deciphering this really isn't all that difficult, it just takes a little work.

To avoid this hassle, you can get a paper like the financial journals I mentioned earlier. Business journals go above and beyond a simple quote. *Investor's Business Daily* actually rates the stocks based on the strength of their earnings. *The Wall Street Journal* offers simple stock quotes, but there's enough business information to make you squeal. A crafty thing that the *Journal* does is draw pictures of people, instead of using photographs, to accompany stories. Each drawing is a piece of art, and I've saved a couple that have caught my attention. My favorite piece in my collection is the sketch of Ronald McDonald.

Magazines: Newspapers with Eye Candy

Besides newspapers, which come daily, you can get magazines and periodicals about investing. These come every week or every month. Since they don't come as quickly as the paper, the weekly periodicals are behind in the news, like a clock that's slow. Perhaps the most well-known publication is *Barron's*, the only major weekly periodical.

I don't like it. In all of my attempts to read it, I've failed. Sometimes I go to the library and sit down and decide, "I'm going to take an hour and thoroughly read *Barron's*." It never happens. I need about half of a full-size table just to unfold the magazine. Not only is the magazine excessively thick, it's messily bound, and I spend half my time reading and the other half putting the paper back together. When I finally get down to reading, the articles are two or three full pages each (tiny print). I just don't have the attention span to deal with that! And a lot of times, each article is chock-full of statistics and numbers—minutiae that isn't all that important.

For example, say the author's talking about the economy. Not only does he tell you about important stuff like how fast the economy's growing, but he also throws in fifteen other statistics about the economy. Then, the author finishes the story by being a chicken. He'll use the "while . . . another" construction to make sure you're totally confused about the issue at hand. An article might finish, "While John Jones, the most successful investor in the world, likes the prospect of this company, another expert, Charlotte Doe, one of the most respected names on Wall Street, thinks the company will go bankrupt within the next three years." It waffles—not much different from the television shows that feature two opposing experts. So, thoroughly confused, I give up on my goal of finishing *Barron's*.

With weekly magazines, you have only a week to get through a big piece of newsprint. But with monthly or biweekly magazines, you have more time. I like to take things apart piece by piece, so I enjoy these types of magazines. And there are so many. But for the new investor, some may be really intimidating. A good starter magazine is *Money*. It's written in simple English, and it doesn't have a lot of financial jargon. It explains everything well. But all these magazines have a tendency to worry about the short term too much. Of course, that's their lifeblood—they have to worry about the short term or they wouldn't have anything to write about. Still, you have to watch out for too much interpretation of the news.

Another fine publication is *Fortune* magazine. It's read by a number of millionaires, so you can consider yourself in good company if you subscribe. It's got the stuff the rich guy reads—the classical-music CD recommendations and business book reviews—but it's really engaging. The thing I like about this magazine is that it's about people more than the markets. If you're interested in money, who has it, and who's getting it, this is the magazine for you. *Fortune* isn't limited to money, but everything's at least partially related to business. There are articles on everything from spies for drug companies to political races. Since the magazine doesn't focus on numbers, there aren't as many charts and graphs as in the newspaper. When there are graphs they're readable, they're in color, and, best of all, they're simple. Even more, there are pictures. All this eye candy makes *Fortune* much more fun than your average newspaper.

Fortune is most famous for the Fortune 500. The Fortune 500 is a list of the largest companies in America based on revenue. Revenue doesn't require much calculation—it's the total amount of money brought in before expenses. If you subtract expenses from revenues, you get profits. I think profits are a more accurate reflection of a company's health, but *Fortune* has been ranking companies by revenues for years. As the reputation of the Fortune 500 has grown, *Fortune* has included other rankings in its listing. Each of the 500 companies is ranked by profitability as well as revenue growth, stock price increases, and other factors.

There are so many other magazines that it's overwhelming to try to read everything. Don't. The library is full of business magazines, and I sometimes try to read all of them. I convince myself that it's useful to read every article on every page, otherwise I miss something. But that's hooey. If, for example, I had never read about the Internet in 1994 or 1995 when it was really beginning to take off, I could have read about it in 1996 or 1997. Nothing important happens so fast that you miss it in a blink of an eye. Most magazines are clones. What you get in one is often found in the other. So if you don't like *Fortune* or *Money,* you may find *Forbes* to be of some interest. And if you want a lot of dry information that might be useful for a term paper, you can read *The Economist.* It's up to you, but believe me, you aren't missing much by not reading them all.

Books: The Secret of Learning

I was talking to a person who works behind a counter at a fast-food restaurant. During the slow times of the day, he walks around aimlessly, bouncing a tennis ball. I said, "You look bored. Why don't you read?" He said, "Reading is *more* boring!" If he only knew the possibilities of reading, he wouldn't be stuck working at a minimum-wage job.

Most teenagers don't like reading. I can see why. The teacher says, "You have to read your textbook to such-and-such page." That's a complete drag, since reading the textbook is like watching molasses drip from bark. So teenagers associate all reading with textbook reading, which it isn't. As Apple says, "Think different."

I'm a complete book nerd. That's why I wrote a book. I learned almost everything I know about stocks and investing and wealth from books. Books allow you to borrow from the experience of many people. You get to know what others have spent years learning. Imagine that you never had an instructor of any kind to teach you how to drive. Wouldn't it be almost impossible to learn? The same is true with investing. If you had to learn about everything yourself, it would be almost impossible.

There's a catch to reading investing books. If you read a number of books on the subject, you'll find that many contradict each other. Everybody has a different take on investing. Even I have a take on investing that's particular to me. Always ask yourself, "Is this person a professional writer or an investor?" Unfortunately, there's an abundance of investment books by professional writers and a shortage of books by professional investors. Professional investors are wary to give out their secrets, especially when those secrets have helped them make a lot of money. Giving them out would be as silly as Coke publishing their secret formula for the general good. There is one major litmus test for professional writers: Does that person make more money writing than investing? You can find out a lot just by reading the jacket of a book. If someone has managed a successful mutual fund for several years and then decides to write a book, it's probably a good bet that you'll find something worthwhile in that book. Professional writers, on the other hand, make the majority of their money through bestsellers and seminars.

Reading books by professional investors or about professional investors can be very enlightening. Near the end of this book, there's a chapter about my odyssey through the book world. It was rather slow and painful, and it took me a while to make sense of every book I read. Ultimately, I learned that there are many paths you can follow to achieve similar successful results. You'll notice, for example, that a couple of the books I've read are by Peter Lynch. Peter Lynch is a professional investor, and an exception to the rule that mutual funds are bad. Even though the fund he ran—Fidelity Magellan—has several hundred million dollars in assets, he still managed to make it grow. That's the kind of person you want to read about. Some books on the list are about Warren Buffett. He's the second richest man in this country, and he happened to accumulate his wealth through buying businesses. I've received a lot of inspiration in my investing from the ideas of Buffett and Lynch, but they aren't carbon copies. Follow Buffett, a guy who made billions in the market, or Lynch, not a book by Dr. Schmo, the Harvard economist who hasn't made a dollar in the markets.

In the end, you've got to go out there and start investing yourself. But books will form a foundation of knowledge that you can use to deal with changes in the market. For example, if the market goes down for a long period of time, you may see that as an opportunity to purchase stock. Since you probably have limited experience in the stock market, you wouldn't have known to do this without reading a book. You're borrowing knowledge from somebody else who knows how to do something and using that to your benefit to make money. I find that very cool.

The Internet: Beam Me Up

I heard Charles Schwab, who owns a big brokerage house called (take a wild guess . . .) Charles Schwab, say, "The Internet is the final . . . empowerment of the individual." Final empowerment, final frontier, final whatever, the Internet is a powerful tool for the individual investor. Information that a wealthy few paid thousands for just a few years ago is available for free via the Internet today. Best of all, finding that information is easy, and everything is paperless.

In the last chapter, we talked about how to use the Internet to save and invest and pay virtually nothing. Now let's talk about how you can use the Internet to find lots of important information. You're probably very familiar with the Internet. Many friends of mine use it every day. There's nothing wrong with that: I use the telephone every day, and now I'm using the Internet every day, too. The thing about investing online is that you can experience information overload. When you choose a brokerage through which you invest your money, you'll find that they may *overload* you with services: stock quotes, stock charts, real-time quotes, everything you don't need.

Fish for the gems and wipe them off. You'll find that several services are good, but very few are great. Here they are:

Quote.yahoo.com

Yahoo! is the best financial portal on the Internet. A portal, by the way, is a site that allows you to go to other sites. Yahoo! itself doesn't have much information, but it connects to other sites that do. At Yahoo! Finance, there's enough information to overload every brain cell you have. They've kept the basics—stock quotes and charts—and they've moved on to everything from interest rate calculators to insurance quotes. Of course, the average teenager doesn't have to worry about insurance or home loans—yet.

The inside skinny on Yahoo! is that it's the fastest site on the net. Even though it gets zillions of hits per day, the people who run it manage to make it lightning-quick to use, even if you have a slow connection. When you first load the site, there's a text box near the top where you can enter any number of ticker symbols. For example, entering "MSFT GE INTC" will give you quotes like the one you saw in the stocks chapter for Microsoft, General Electric, and Intel. Actually, the quote we used a couple of chapters ago was an extended quote similar to a Yahoo! quote. The nice thing about Yahoo! is that you can pull up a company, and they've got the whole scoop on it. Near the name of the company you can click on a profile of it and see how much money the company makes and other interesting numbers.

I must warn you, however, about Yahoo! and other sites with message boards. The Internet is chock-full of message boards—places where people write and respond to each other where the world can see—and there's a lot of rumor and fear on these boards. Don't read the messages. If you do, don't trust anything anybody says. A lot of people are willing to lie to get others to buy the stock. And even if they aren't lying, people on these boards are forever arguing. I've read posts on these boards many times, and they sound more like two people fighting on Jerry Springer than two intelligent investors. One will write, "You are obviously a moron. You know nothing about XYZ company, and I do. It's great." And the other will come back and say, "Dumb fool! XYZ's going to tank, and I'm going to watch you sink." It's not very civil, and there's no purpose in you joining them. Otherwise, Yahoo! is a fine place to find information.

Rapid Research, www.rapidresearch.com

There are very few *really good* sites dealing with what's called "fundamental research." If you play sports, you know the fundamentals are the basic shots—the jump shot in basketball or the forehand in tennis. In investing, the fundamentals are equally important. They're the financial information that composes the core of the company. This includes terms that we've already discussed before, like the earnings per share, return on equity, assets, liabilities, and other important figures. Up to now, we've just discussed their dictionary definitions. In Chapter 7, we'll really go in depth and see how you can use the information from the site to make money.

Most important, Rapid Research allows you to screen stocks. That means you can enter certain criteria—price-to-earnings ratio, size, return on equity, and other figures—and get a list of companies that fit these criteria. For example, you can write that the P/E ratio should be a maximum of twenty. All the stocks that come up will have a ratio of twenty or less. If you do this with several criteria, your results will be small, but valuable. Panning for gold requires sifting through a lot of water and dirt.

Free Annual Reports, www.annualreportservice.com

One of the finest services on the Internet, this site provides **annual reports**. Every public company is legally required to release an annual report, which is a statement of operations that includes a financial report and usually very straightforward information from management. If you read these reports carefully, you'll find more information than you can imagine. You can make inferences from the quality of the report and how highly the management sings its own praises. We'll discuss annual reports in more depth later, but remember their importance.

There are over 3,000 companies that participate in this service. If you find that you're in need of information about a company that doesn't participate in the service, check out their Web site. If you can't find it on their Web site, give them a ring. Whether you use the Internet, the telephone, the mail, or the public library, find the annual report and read it.

Smart Money Market Map, www.smartmoney.com/marketmap

This is, by far, the coolest financial site on the net. It's a visual representation of the market. Each industry—technology, finance, health care—is represented by a square. Some industry squares are larger than others, denoting how big an industry is compared to others. For example, technology is *very large* compared to finance or health care. Within each industry, squares of varying sizes represent companies that are part of that industry. For example, within technology, Microsoft is represented by a huge square. Or in consumer staples (sometimes known as the junk food industry), Coca-Cola takes up about three quarters of the market compared to one quarter for Pepsi. Click on any company and you can zoom in on a more detailed market map of that specific industry. What's more, the color of each company gives you a clue about that sector and the market in general. The lighter the red, the more stocks have fallen. On the other end of the spectrum, the lighter the green, the more stocks have risen. If you zoom out to the total market, you can see how well (or poorly) it does each day. This is a dynamic site.

Morningstar, www.morningstar.net

Morningstar is an excellent site for analysis. Each company is thoroughly surveyed, and Morningstar appraises the value of each stock as a business, a philosophy I believe in. Later we'll talk about how to look at the business behind the stock and see if the two are in line. Morningstar allows you to cheat—at least just a little—by letting them do all the work for you.

Vault Reports, www.vault.com

I like to find information on companies anywhere I can. One of the best sources is people who actually work for those companies. Vault.com offers reports about companies for prospective employees. About 3,000 employers are listed, and there are 8,000 public companies, meaning that only well-known companies are listed. If you're researching at least a relatively well-known company, I suggest you go to this Web site. The site provides a free message board for employees to complain about or praise their company. These message boards allow you to gauge company culture. Culture isn't tangible, but it fits directly into one of the factors we'll look at later—the ability of the management. Incompetent management never creates good culture, and employees will be more than happy to complain.

Some of the information I've learned from this Web site has influenced my decisions considerably. I discovered that one company I researched had laid off 80% of the workers in one of its subsidiaries. People weren't working up to their potential because they were plain scared of being fired. Even though the company's numbers were as solid as could be, I didn't think that they had the right long-term idea.

Investor's Business Daily, www.investors.com

A well-known secret on the Internet is that you don't have to buy the morning newspaper anymore. *The New York Times, The Los Angeles Times, The Washington Post,* and other prestigious publications can be found on-line, the full editions are available at your fingertips. But for the average young investor, reading the business section of these newspapers is like listening to a broken record. You don't need to hear the same thing over and over again. And you don't need full-page articles about everything. In fact, many of the newspapers get their news feeds from similar sources—Reuters and the Associated Press, for example—so when I say that they're all saying the same thing, they actually may be. Also, if you're entering college any time soon, you may be able to get a free electronic version of papers like *The Wall Street Journal* on-line. Check it out.

What's nice about the on-line version of *IBD* is that you don't have to pay for it, and it's simple and fast to read. Once you get into the actual paper (click on "Read Today's Edition"), you can look at the Top Ten, which are summaries of the major news items of the day. You can read all the items about new industries and people doing exciting things. It's good, clean Internet fun.

Summary: In this chapter, we learned . . .
- There are several ways to gather information about money and investing. In fact, if anything, there's an overload of news.
- Television business news is too short-term-oriented, and most of the information deals with the rapid fluctuations in stock prices.

- Newspapers offer a broad overview of the market, and they're deeper and more informative than television.
- Magazines are visually pleasing but packed with a lot of useless information. Weekly magazines are an even larger overload.
- Books are a fine way to learn, but only if you read the right authors. Near the end of this book we will discuss other good reads.
- The internet offers free, easy access to all the information you need.

PART II

Investing Your
Hard-Earned Cash

6

An Intro to Making Money on the Street

Enough background—it's time to make money! There are very few important principles when it comes to investing. In fact, three things count in investing: Make the most money, make it fast, and make it consistently with as little risk as possible. If we were perfect, we could do all three all the time. But we aren't. We have to sacrifice one for another and balance them.

As a young investor, you can make a lot of money, and you can minimize your risk, but you can't do it quickly. To make money quickly is to take a huge risk and a large chunk of time. Unless you are willing to devote your life to trading, that risk isn't the correct choice. Instead, think logically. Think in the long term.

Sure, buying and selling stocks quickly has its advantages. This is called trading. If you do it correctly, you have the potential to make a lot of money, and more rapidly than if you invest for the long term. Day trading, trading taken to its extreme, offers the best opportunities to make money. But there's a caveat to that—you have to be *really good* or you'll fall flat on your face. You may have heard of day trading in the news. The technology available today has allowed investors to make many trades in a day relatively cheaply. Remember how commissions in the past used to be $100 per trade? That was stifling to most people. Today, though, commissions range between $5 and $30. At $5, it costs a total of ten dollars to buy and sell a stock, and trades can be executed at lightning speeds. You don't need to call up a broker; the speed at which you enter an order is limited only by how fast you can type.

Day traders use technology to try to capture small price jumps. While this may seem appealing, more and more people have entered the game, so it's really tough to play. In fact, some people estimate that

70% of all day traders are unsuccessful. And those who ultimately turn a profit usually lose a lot of cash in their first six months. This is not a good game for you! I figure that those who turn a profit have some kind of trading experience, and it often takes them six months to get adjusted to the game. Don't be arrogant and think that you'll fare any better.

I now preach the gospel of long-term investing, although I've unsuccessfully tried to trade for the short term in the past. I started believing in it faithfully after I decided that I'd forgo some profits in order to be relieved of the stress. I've also discovered many other benefits besides a relaxed attitude toward investing. One of them is that I've learned a tremendous amount about business. Wall Street is a gateway to understanding business. Business is the art of making money—nothing else. And if you learn to understand this art, you'll be able to thrive in your career even if you never invest a dime. Over the next few chapters, you'll see how to analyze businesses. This is something I never knew how to do before I began investing. And it's certainly affected my career aspirations. It will change yours, too. You may find that you have a knack for this kind of thinking, and that it may be possible for you to start your own business.

Another benefit of long-term investing is delayed taxes. Taxes keep popping up; they're a recurring nightmare. The government finds great ways to waste the money you give it, and I'd love to forget about taxes. Still, I prefer my home to jail. So it's a real concern, and taxes benefit the long-term investor *far* more than the trader. An excellent trader may make a 50% return in one year, for example. That means he takes $100,000 and turns it into $150,000. By any rate, that's an outstanding return! But he has to give up to a fifth of the profits to the government, because he bought and then he sold. That means he makes only $34,000 during the year, for a total of $134,000.

But if you have a stock, and it goes up 25% one year and you don't sell, you get to keep that profit. You're now $25,000 richer on paper, without having to pony up to the government. You only have to pay when you sell. In this case, I'd forget about the $9,000 I didn't make just so I don't have to worry about the daily fluctuations in price. Besides, 50% is unreal. Returns like that rarely happen. Certainly, good returns take skill and luck, and a more realistic goal for a new investor is 20% or 25% a year.

I was watching CNBC one day, and there was a debate between two people. One was a successful investor and the other was a trader who specialized in high-risk technology stocks. The investor had a twenty-year track record of success, and the trader, while successful, had been working for only three years. They argued for five minutes before the investor made a crucial statement to his colleague: "I invest, you gamble."

I invest, you gamble. Investors make informed decisions. They purchase a stake in a company not in hopes of quickly selling it by the end of the week, but in hopes of the company becoming the finest company in its industry. They hope it can become the finest company on the stock market. Investors invest in businesses. Gamblers buy and sell stocks. Here's another Liebowitz Law:

Investing involves buying a business. When you choose an investment, choose it as if you were buying the underlying business. That means looking at two important factors: the quality of the business and the price.

The process of investing is similar to buying a car. However, instead of just looking at the nicely washed exterior, I'll teach you how to examine the engine, the tires, and all the parts. I'll also show you whether you have a Mercedes or a Pinto. And perhaps most important, I'll teach you what price you should pay.

Quality and price apply to everything. They are, for example, how Donald Trump buys real estate. In December 1995, *The Wall Street Journal* reported that he bought 40 Wall Street for $1 million. He was able to do that because the real estate market was horrible. Real estate, like stocks, moves in cycles. Sometimes the waves of greed and euphoria are washing in, and sometimes they're washing out. In this case, nobody could manage the building. Trump renovated the building. In 1998, the first year it was open, his profits exceeded $20 million.

You'll pull the same tricks. Sometimes the stock market will be riddled with fear. At one point during the mini-depression that hit between 1972 and 1973, the value of collectible postage stamps increased faster than the Dow. Talk about pathetic. But that was a period of fear that meant a buying opportunity. And, of course, the market picked up. In the seventeen years since 1982, the market has grown upward of 1300%. Trouble often means opportunity—if you know how to spot it.

Most people on Wall Street care about one thing: the price of the stock going up. The truth is, however, that this is a secondary concern. If the company is excellent, the price will always rise. Just like Donald Trump's real estate in Manhattan, the cream rises to the top in stock investments.

Summary: In this chapter, we learned . . .
- Business perspective investing: Think of stocks as business, not as something you want to buy and sell within a month.
- In any purchase, two concerns are important: Quality and price. Buy quality businesses at low prices.
- The stock market has waves of good performance and bad performance. While it's almost impossible to predict when a good stretch or bad stretch will hit, it's possible to purchase good companies when stocks are in a slump, knowing that the slump won't last forever.

Finding Your Perfect Company

There's no perfect company—sorry. There's no perfect group of companies—I apologize again. But there are exceptional companies. There are companies that have the potential to grow for long periods of time. There are companies that are changing the way we think about the world.

For years, if people went into a restaurant, they'd have to wait twenty minutes or longer until their food was served. Today, McDonald's will serve you a meal in less than one and a half minutes. Once upon a time, a package delivered in three days was fast. Federal Express came along and changed all that, and today a package can be delivered from Los Angeles to New York overnight. Dell can make you a custom computer at a great price and ship it in less than two weeks. Technology is always changing, and great companies are always emerging.

How do you find these companies? Are they good long-term investments? The answers are clear: These companies are wonderful investments for the long term, and they're everywhere. You can find great companies by reading. I've read articles in *Fortune* and *The Wall Street Journal*, and I've been blown away by what some companies are doing. Read as much as you can. Find companies that are doing amazing things.

After that, always read their annual report. Every public company produces an annual report. It's an overview of the company, listing all of its operations and activities. Securities law requires companies to reveal negatives about themselves, so by reading the reports, you should be able to make an informed decision.

To start, we begin with the six key elements of a good company.

1. Great Economics

Some businesses work and some don't. **Economics**, as we refer to them, are the factors that make a company financially great. A company *must* have some kind of stronghold on its industry. That means that people almost *have* to use their products. On the Internet, to connect computers, Cisco Systems dominates. Everyone who buys a PC gets Microsoft software. Coca-Cola dominates the soft-drink business. In each of these cases, the business has some kind of monopoly. People aren't choosing to use the products of the business because they are cheap; in fact, they may be more expensive than the rest. Ask yourself: What products do I know that people either have to use or choose to use even if they're more expensive?

Companies that can charge more have a "brand name." Brand names are worth gold. They're a mental shortcut. If you want a computer, you can search around on the Internet for a good computer, or you can go to Dell Computer. They're a brand. An excellent example of how powerful brands are is the drug industry. If you walk into a drugstore, you'll find that you can buy either Tylenol or acetaminophen. Tylenol is the brand name, acetaminophen is the generic product. Generic products have the same ingredients, but they're cheaper than most brand-name drugs because the store that sells them packages them. By all accounts, they're the same thing at a cheaper price. But brand names like Tylenol control 93% of the drug market, while generic products have only 7%. Brand names work, and new ones are always developing. Some brand names aren't known to the general public. For example, chances are you haven't heard of Trilogy Software, but it's a brand name in business-to-business software. There's a good chance this stock may be the next Microsoft.

Another element of a company with great economics is its ability to raise prices without people ceasing to buy the product. You already know that drug companies can charge more for their products. Microsoft is another example. They've raised the price of their Office software without taking a hit in sales. Why is this good? It means the company has such a sound product that it doesn't need to lower its price to sell product. It just sells itself.

Some companies just can't say that. Airlines, for example, have a tough time creating brands. Very few people are willing to pay higher prices for more service. Price wars happen constantly. One company will cut prices, then a string of companies will follow. It's fantastic for travelers, but investors have seen the stocks of airline companies produce mediocre returns in the last ten years. Competitive as they are, airlines are lucky to break even and generate marginally positive returns for their investors.

What companies have good economics? That's often based on the industry. In the previous example of airlines, the one basic function of an airline is to take you from point A to point B. Airline travelers definitely want kind flight attendants, but they aren't willing to pay that much for them. Some industries, on the other hand, allow a company to define itself better. For example, a speaker system is a rather scientific device that converts signals from some source into sound waves. But there's a lot of opportunity for companies in this industry to make a name for themselves. Bose has created a name by producing very small speakers with a high quality of sound. On top of that, they've priced the speakers high enough to eliminate lower-income buyers. My Japanese-manufactured clock radio costs $50, but a Bose system goes for seven times that amount, yet Bose hasn't suffered one iota. Indeed, they've prospered from this strategy. That's a powerful enough brand to whet the appetite of any investor.

2. Good People Behind the Wheel

The most difficult part of any task is getting the right people to do it. Have you ever had a class project to do with a group of four people, and you're the only one who wants to work? Don't worry, it doesn't just happen to you. I'm always amazed by the masses of people who have no interest in anything. They plod along aimlessly, content with mediocrity. They're definitely not the people I'd want running my company. Nor are they the people I want running companies that I own—even if I have only one share of their company.

With my strict criteria, I really have to weed out a lot of good companies with bad management. However, I find that it's always for the better: even the best horse can't win with a bad jockey. So, what kind of manager should you look for? And how do you find out if someone is the best? Before anything, make sure the company has sound economics. Good managers can improve a bad business, but they can't make it a great business. I'll give you an example. Tower Records started as a small company that catered mainly to college students. They managed to create a monstrous empire out of a string of small stores. However, I would never invest in Tower Records, only because the music business has bad economics. People are flocking to buy cheap music at CDNow.com. There are as many price wars in the music industry as there are in the airline industry. People want their favorite CDs for the cheapest price, and nothing anybody can do will stop them—even wonderful management.

If the company has good economics, then look for honest, innovative management. You'll find that some management is overly optimistic about the future of their company. You can often spot their tone in their annual reports. You'll see some management has enough integrity to tell the truth. But watch out for the CEO who makes his business seem like it's strong enough to take over the world. Positive comments are okay, but if the dominant theme is congratulatory, this executive is a salesman, not an honest person. If he's not honest with the shareholders, he's not honest with the company's problems. All companies have problems, and they should be addressed in the letter to the shareholders.

Another issue is the creativity of the management. Some managers are lemmings: they all jump over the cliff together. For example, as of this writing, a number of companies were making "investments" in Internet companies. I wrote an article for a popular financial Web site entitled "Lemmings.com." I wrote how disappointed I was in Starbucks and AOL for making investments in unprofitable Internet companies. Starbucks has an excellent core business (and ultimately I said it would turn out okay) in gourmet coffee, but it was investing in a Web site that sold furniture and other household items over the Internet. Ugh! Not only was Starbucks venturing away from a business that it knew, it was going into a business with very little profit (we'll talk about the importance of profits later). The management disappointed me: To me, they were trying to make a quick buck by investing in the Internet and boosting their stock price. It's okay to do that if the business is a sound one, but retailing on the Internet is far from secure and profitable. Most companies fail at it. AOL, on a similar note, had just paid $100 million for a company which produces a software program that plays MP3 files, a popular music format. The company gives away the software for free, and while I respect the company and its products, it doesn't make money *at all*. Charities make more than this company. AOL had bought it and many other Web sites, but I didn't see any financial reasons for these decisions. Ask yourself: Is the company expanding into low-profit or high-profit businesses?

The people behind the wheel should have the ability to innovate. They should actively pursue different opportunities. I like management that ventures into different areas—with, of course, the expectation of profit from those ventures; otherwise, they all turn out to be misadventures. Starbucks can't expect a good profit from selling furniture on the Internet. Yet some companies honestly do search for profits that will help shareholder value. What first attracted me to Microsoft was their ability to venture into different areas and strengthen the ones that have been most profitable. Business is about taking educated risks. We talked about that in the first chapter: Ultimately, success is the result of taking risk.

Jim Clark, the founder of three successful companies in Silicon Valley—the hotspot of competition between computer companies—talks all the time about taking a risk to serve a market. But Microsoft takes that to another level. They've ventured into joysticks, keyboards, Web sites, and Web browsers. They've strengthened what has been successful, such as their Web sites, which are the most profitable on the Internet. And they've limited their efforts in joysticks and other "peripherals" in which they haven't been as successful. Management is willing to take a risk. Of course, they know that if they take a loss, they have billions of dollars of profit from other sources to cushion them.

To find out the spirit of the management, read the letter to their shareholders, which can be found at the beginning of the annual report. There's no other document that looks as far forward. Read about the company. If you can see that the wind has changed direction and the company forgot to turn their sails, watch out. We'll take a look at examples of companies who can change and those who can't. The Liebowitz Law about this is as follows:

Management needs to be innovative, but the company must have a consistent history.

Even though Microsoft, for example, ventures into new territory that has profit potential, it still rakes in billions from the core business of selling its Windows operating system and other software. That's been a consistent moneymaker for the company. When we look at a case study in the next chapter, you'll be able to understand what I mean about management more fully. Their skill can make or break your decision to invest in the company. At this point, you may be overwhelmed by what it takes to invest. Remember, however, by doing all this work you put yourself at a huge advantage over everyone else—who are, compared to you, simply throwing darts at a board.

3. The Numbers: Great Profit Margins

In business, profits are king. In a great business, **profit margins** are king. Remember what profits are: how much money you bring in minus how much money you pay out. Profit margins are a percentage that's independent of how large profits are. Margins are how much profit you make divided by your expenses. For example, if I sold you a coffee machine for $120, and that coffee machine cost me $100, I'd make $20 in profit. The profit margin would be 20% (20 ÷ 100). That's a great profit margin and a sign of a healthy business. Note that the same would be true if, for example, you sold a plane for $12 million that only cost you $10 million. That $2 million profit would still translate into a 20% profit margin.

Margins tell you more than any other economic figure. A company with high margins may have a monopoly hold on an industry, which is definitely a good thing for you. They can charge high prices for their product and get away with it. They can continue to raise prices without taking a hit. If you want a quick check of this, go to www.rapidresearch.com. As a test, enter CSCO, Cisco Systems, as the ticker symbol. Click on "Complete Fundamental Report." Notice that their margins are about 17%. That's outstanding, and it gives a clue that their core business is excellent. And that's the case. Cisco, as you know, makes routers for the Internet, products that virtually no one else makes as well as they do.

On the other hand, I've never recommended a company like Wal-Mart. Wal-Mart is the chain superstore that sells thousands of items. They sell at low prices, prices so low they aren't much above what the company paid for the product. Soap you buy for $3 may have cost them $2.50. However, Wal-Mart has so many locations that the $.50 they make is multiplied tens of thousands of times. Still, the profit margins are dismal. They range from 2% to 4%. That doesn't leave much room for error. The company is walking a tightrope without a net. Wal-Mart has created a brand name, but I doubt they've created brand loyalty. Their brand name comes from their price, not their quality.

4. Little or No Debt

Have you ever eaten with a person who just doesn't stop? He finishes the food on his plate and then takes food off your plate. Not surprisingly, he's fat. He can't move very far, and he's weighed down when he tries to do anything athletic. There are a lot of companies that are weighed down like this. Run as far away from them as you can. Specifically, many companies use **debt**, or **leverage**, which is the art of using other people's money to buy things. You or your parents may use debt every day in the form of the credit card. If you have a big balance with the company that you have to struggle to pay off, you know how damaging debt can be. Unfortunately, a lot of companies use other people's money very well.

During the 1980s, an astonishing eating binge rocked finance: junk bonds. **Bonds** are financial instruments that allow you to lend money up front to get money back in the future. The money you receive in the future is called the **interest payment** or coupon payment, and your return on investment from the bond is called the **yield**. We'll talk about bonds in much greater detail in Chapter 11, but it suffices to say that you can choose to invest in government or corporate bonds. Junk bonds are a type of corporate bond. The company is taking money up front and promising to pay it back later with interest. In other words, you may invest $1,000 at the beginning of the year in a corporate bond with an interest rate of 7%. At the end of the year, you'd expect to receive $1,070, your principal ($1,000) plus interest ($70). For the most part, corporate bonds are *high quality*. There's a really good chance that you can get your money back plus interest. That wasn't the case with junk bonds.

To understand that, let's look at bonds from the flip side—from the corporation's view. The company is taking money now and promising to pay it back later. That interest is a liability, and so the company that uses debt is in debt—at some point, they're going to have to pay it off. But during the 1980s and the early 1990s, a number of companies used the proceeds from the sale of these bonds—a stratospheric amount, somewhere near a trillion dollars—to buy other companies. They thought, "Well, gee, let's buy this company, and this company, and this company, and hopefully we can use the profits to pay back the bond-holders."

The main attraction of these bonds to individuals like you and me was their high interest rates. Junk bonds yield 14–15%. That's as much as you have to pay on your credit card bills. But imagine all these companies having to pay back billions of dollars in debt, plus interest payments of 15%! It's almost impossible. It made a small number of people very rich, since all of a sudden they had control of large corporations. These **corporate raiders** became so famous the movie *Wall Street* was based on their adventures. Ultimately, in their greed, they caused a lot of havoc and wreckage. The new owners had to sell parts of the companies. For example, Revlon had to sell off many of its profitable makeup divisions to other companies just to pay back their creditors. And they couldn't pay back a lot of the debt. A number of companies couldn't pay the interest on their junk bonds and went bankrupt. In fact, Drexel Burnham Lambert, once a prestigious investment firm, collapsed because the companies it helped finance couldn't pay back what they owed Drexel. The moral of the story: Debt stinks.

Look for companies that have little or no debt. You probably won't find many companies without *any* debt. Companies that have a 0 in the debt column slap you in the face. They're striking. Something's really spectacular about the company. It isn't bad to have debt, but it should be justified. Debt shouldn't be more than a third of the assets. We've talked about assets, but to refresh your memory, they are anything that puts money in your pocket. Wal-Mart, for example, counts its stores as assets, since they generate large amounts of profits. If debt is as large or larger than the assets a company has, that spells trouble: The company is already in the hole. In order to succeed, they have to work out of the hole. You want a company with a sure thing, a great product—a company that isn't clawing its way to survive.

5. Excellent Returns on Equity

Equity is a fancy term for how much a company is worth. It's the assets minus the liabilities. You can find out how much equity you have by seeing how many assets you have—like savings accounts and such—and how much you owe. Of course, compared to some companies, the amount of equity we have is peanuts. Some corporations have billions in equity, which is a wonderful thing, but that doesn't help you much.

You want to see the company grow, you want to see it expand, and you want to see what is called a **return on equity (ROE)**. Return on equity is simple: it's the earnings of the company divided by the equity. For example, if a company has $10 million in equity and makes $2 million, that's a 20% return on equity. You're probably saying now, "Why do we have to use all these ratios? It's getting to be a little much." There are so many ratios out there, we're only at the tip of the iceberg! Most are a lot of unnecessary arithmetic, and we're only interested in a few. If a company has an ROE of 15% or 20%, it means that for every $1 they earn, the company is investing it to get back $1.15 or $1.20. That's beautiful. You know that the company is kicking it up a notch when they get that kind of return.

I consider ROE an excellent way to judge management. Why? We'll work it out with an example. Pretend you own some apartments in New York. People pay you rents to live in these buildings. For the first $10 million you invest in these buildings, you earn $3 million in first-year profits. This gives a 30% ROE ($3 million divided by $10 million). You purchase some more buildings for another $10 million. Now you have $20 million worth of buildings. This year, though, you earn $4 million. Your ROE has dropped from 30% to 20%($4 million divided by $20 million). This isn't necessarily that bad, but if it happens consistently to any company you invest in, you're probably investing in a bad manager, especially if the ROE is low to begin with. They buy expensive assets, but those assets don't generate good returns for them.

You may see a company double its earnings every year, but the ROE goes down. These are companies with great businesses and poor management. Many people measure a company by how fast it can grow its earnings. Often, companies want to maintain the rapid pace of growth, and so they buy a lot of other companies. These acquisitions boost earnings, but return on equity falls. If you see that in a company report, it shows that company has bitten off a bigger piece than it can chew. By the way, earnings are measured as earnings per share (EPS). EPS is the total earnings divided by the number of shares. In this example, we'll see where earnings have grown but returns on equity have fallen. Take a look at the following chart:

NOT-SO-GREAT COMPANY, INC.

| Earnings per Share | | | | |
1995	1996	1997	1998	1999
1.00	1.50	2.25	3.38	5.07

For the last five years, this great company has increased its earnings by 50%. Each year, earnings are 50% higher than the last year. Most financial people who saw this would be filled with joy. I'm not so excited. Here's why:

NOT-SO-GREAT COMPANY, INC.

| Return on Equity | | | | |
1995	1996	1997	1998	1999
30%	20%	17%	12%	9%

As the years progressed, management got worse. They weren't able to keep up the great returns on equity. And how can you possibly expect to keep up 50% earnings growth forever? That means the company would double its earnings in less than two years. Within thirty years the company would have more money than exists in the world! This is absurd. Don't worry about speed. Worry about consistency. I measure consistency by return on equity.

6. Consistent Earnings

Earnings are important, but people make far too much of a fuss over them. What are earnings? They're profits. They're the total sales of a company subtracted by the costs. And they're an absolute number, taken out of context. That means that if I told you a company made $20 million this year, you'd say, "Wow." But if I told you that same company made $120 million last year, you'd say, "Ugh." Earnings dropped $100 million.

Few companies have the ability to keep their earnings growing. This is an impressive task. If you can find people who can do it, invest in their companies. Consistency doesn't mean speed. It means a gradual climb uphill. Earnings that go from $.50 to $1.00 to $2.50 to $1.25 to $.80 aren't good earnings. Earnings that go from $.50 to $.80 to $1.00 to $1.25

to $2.50 are. Over a five-year stretch, both companies have made the same *total* amount of money, but each has taken a different path.

Another note about earnings: Make sure you're not investing in an industry that has to spend a lot of its earnings just to keep everything running smoothly. Airlines are an example of an industry that has to spend huge amounts to do this. They have to buy new planes when the old ones wear out, and they have to spend large sums maintaining these planes. On the other hand, many new technology industries, like the Internet or the software industry, don't have to purchase new equipment or update heavy machinery. Microsoft, for example, has to buy a new computer once in a while. Web sites may have to purchase a new server on occasion, but very little money in general goes to equipment.

Some companies choose to pay a part of these earnings as dividends, some choose to reinvest it. I'm much stricter with companies that choose to reinvest the income. If the dividend per share is zero, the company must have a high return on equity for me to consider it. That's because if my money is paid out in a dividend, the company is saying: Here, we'll let you invest the money yourself. (When I say invest, it doesn't just mean the stock market; it can be in new equipment, people, or anywhere money could be used to increase the company's profits.) But if they choose to keep the money, they're saying: We're smarter than you, and we can beat the returns our shareholders can get. In other words, the company thinks it's wiser for investors to plow money back into their company instead of investing in other companies.

We'll test to see if this is true. You might find this odd, but make sure you conduct this test to see if (A) management is creating value and (B) the company is balancing dividends and retained earnings well. Let's pretend we have ABC corporation, a big pharmaceutical company. The stock price was $40 at the beginning of the year, and it was $42 by the end. They have 100 million shares of stock, and they make $4 per share in earnings. Of that, they pay out $2 per share in dividends, and they retain, or keep for themselves, the remaining two dollars. Let's say they did this at the beginning of the year.

Here's the test: *If the company can match or exceed retained earnings with the growth in the stock's value, then you have a quality company.* In our example, the company retained $2 per share. That's equal to $200 million. At the same time, the price of the stock went from $20 to $22 per share, signaling a $2-per-share gain. The market value jumped $200 million. In this instance, the company has matched its retained earnings with the growth in the stock price. Clearly, management's done a good job allocating the money it rakes in. In reality, this test is more effective when it's done over a period of years because during some years the price can suffer an unjust hit even if the company hasn't fared that badly. Truly exceptional companies may retain hundreds of millions of dollars over a period of several years, but their market value may exceed that, increasing by billions of dollars.

Summary: In this chapter, we learned . . .

- Annual reports are a key tool to learning about a company. They provide all the information necessary to figure out how the company's doing.
- There are six criteria for finding a company that has both room to grow and a lot of stability in its industry. They are:

Great economics—This is the toughest for the novice investor to judge. A company with good economics can comfortably raise prices and is in an industry that you understand that isn't facing turmoil. Some of the best companies have a virtual monopoly on their product or have a product that people need, like an operating system to run their computer (think Microsoft).

Good management—Honest people with intelligence. Look for them to be candid and good investors in their own right—that is, their ability to invest in other companies through acquisitions as well as their own.

Profit margins—Good margins mean a strong company in a strong industry. Margins are the difference between the product's price and the profit the company makes. Higher margins mean that a company isn't forced to slash its prices.

Little or no debt—A company that isn't in debt is free to grow, invest in itself, or invest in other companies without the obligation of paying down its debt to other people, like creditors.

Returns on equity—An essential trait of a good company is a good return on equity. In a company without much debt, the ROE is roughly equivalent to its growth rate. Watch out for falling returns in companies that are acquiring heavily. That means their acquisitions are making them bulky, but not any better of a company.

Consistent earnings—At first glance you should be able to spot companies that have increased earnings consistently over the past five to ten years. If all of the other above criteria are there, you should expect good growth in the next decade.

Price, Oh Almighty Price
(Math Chapter, Ugh)

I never thought bad clothes would tick me off as much as they do. I went to the department store to buy a Polo shirt that I saw a famous tennis player wearing. It looked cool and comfortable, so I bought it for $50. Within a month, the buttons were falling off. The edges frayed. The shirt shrunk to baby size in the dryer. It was certainly not worth $50. Yet, I would have happily paid $5 for that shirt.

The lesson to learn is that anything and everything has a price tag. The same is true for stocks. All stocks have an appropriate price. And all companies have what's called an **intrinsic value**. You may hear a lot of people on television blab about this number. It just means how much a company is worth. Think about it. We'll draw a parallel to a gumball machine. Let's assume you own a gumball machine. You make $100 a year in profit from this machine. Pretend this money will come in forever. You'll see $100 from this machine this year, and next year, and the year after, and then on until the cows start coming home.

How much are you willing to pay for this machine? The answer is the basis for our tactics in valuing businesses. Once we learn how to value businesses, we can spot stocks that have prices way out of line with their real worth. How would you like to buy a company that's worth $100 million for $20 million? We'll start the education by answering the gumball machine question.

What percentage return do you want the first year? In other words, what would the return on investment (ROI, our old friend Roy) be in the first year? If you put your money in a government bond, you'd make about 6% on your money. If you put your money in a good corporate bond (high quality, remember those?) you'd make about 8%. So you want something more than that. How about 10%? There's got to be a reason to buy this gumball machine over a government or corporate bond, since you're definitely taking a major risk—nobody may like your gumball machine. If you wanted a 10% return, then you'd pay $1000. That means that the first year, the $100 comes rolling in, and you've made 10% return on your money ($100/ $1000). Not bad. Let's say you paid $2000 for the gumball machine. The first year $100 comes in. That's only a 5% return. You could do better investing your money in government bonds, with a guarantee that you'll receive your money. If you paid $500, in the first year you'd make a 20% return. *The price you pay determines your return: the lower the price, the better.*

The same is true in the stock market. People are fearful at times and they're giddy at others. Stocks rarely go up and down proportionally to how well or how poorly a company does. There's always an exaggerated reaction. If a company is doing well, the stock will shoot up. If a company is doing poorly, the stock will drop dramatically. Nothing is sane in the stock market. You can take advantage of that. When prices are down, you can pick up companies that are worth far more than the value the market puts on them. That's like buying at a discount store, but then getting to sell the clothes back to the department store at full price! Unfortunately, you won't be able to *instantly* sell back your goods at full price. The stock will have to go up in price.

So what determines the right price at which to buy? It's a little different than how much you're willing to pay for department-store clothes. And it's more complicated than buying a gumball machine. When it comes to pricing a stock, the question is: How much cash do I pay now for future cash? In other words, how much should I pay *now* for money that the company earns *in the future?*

My purpose in giving you all these criteria for selecting stocks in the last chapter has been to make sure you're dealing with a consistently profitable company. Follow those criteria and you'll find quality companies. Your goal is to find companies with the ability to make money for long periods of time. Only then can you make important decisions about finding the right price.

Before we talk about stocks, let's return to the gumball machine for a moment. In the real world, even gumball machines don't have static returns. Earnings fluctuate, growing or falling. Let's say the machine's earnings grew 20% each year. One hundred dollars the first year increases to $120 in the next year, then to $144, and so on. What's the correct price for this machine? Here's what I'd say: I think you should demand a return on your investment that is at least equal to the current 30-Year Treasury Bond *in the first year*. Now you may ask, "What's a 30-Year Treasury Bond?" When we spoke of junk bonds, we were focusing mainly on corporations. However, the federal government issues debt as well. Their debt is generally perceived to be very safe. The reasoning is simple: If they can't pay it off, they will print it—literally. The 30-Year Treasury Bond is the landmark bond from the federal government, and since it is considered a virtually riskless investment, the interest rate is meager, recently around 6%. I use it as a benchmark to determining the returns on other investments. Since the earnings in the first year in our example will be $100, and the yield on the 30-year bond is about 6%, I'd say you should pay somewhere around $1700 ($100 divided by 6.0%–0.06 on your calculator).

Seventeen hundred dollars is correct, but I don't want to pay that much. If I pay, let's say, $1000, in the first year when earnings are $100, I get an initial return of 10%, or $100 divided by $1000. Since earnings will continue to grow, it's like a bond with an initial return of 8% which will gush more cash in the next year, and the next, and the next. . . .

Now let's turn our attention to the real thing: stocks. We do the same thing with stocks. First we look at the company through the glasses we made in the last chapter. We survey the earnings, the economics, and all the other good things that allow us to say, "Hey, this is a great company. I think it's safe to say it will be around for a while." Then we ask, "How much am I willing to pay?"

This time we aren't talking about gumball machines, however. The first step is to figure out how fast a company can grow. Let's say a company earned $2 billion last year. Unfortunately, unlike a theoretical gumball machine, there's no way to predict how fast earnings will grow tomorrow, next week, or next year, and there's certainly no method to figuring them out for the long term. Most on-line sources, however, will give you the *past* earnings growth rate of a company. Let's say in this example it's 7% (if you're stuck, go to www.rapidresearch.com, and they'll tell you the average EPS growth rate of any company). Estimate next year's earnings: $2 billion x 0.07 (7% growth added to the $2 billion) which is $2.14 billion. Divide by the current bond yield, which is about 6%, or 0.06. That comes out to nearly $36 billion ($2.14 billion ÷ 0.06).

This number is about what you should pay if you wanted to earn a 6% return on investment. To figure out what $36 billion is per share, divide by the number of shares. If there's one billion shares, you'd pay $36 per share. If you paid less—buying at a discount—you'd get a better return on your investment, assuming the earnings remain stable. Or if the earnings make a big jump, you'll get a nice return on investment.

The price you pay is the most important part of the investment equation. The more you pay for any stock relative to its earnings, the more risk you take. In today's market, for example, technology companies are selling at very high prices compared to their profits. As I told you earlier, some Internet companies aren't even making any money. Why would anyone purchase stock in those companies? To speculate. People, in general, think that sometime in the future these companies will generate huge amounts of money. So they buy the stock now in hopes that earnings will pan out in the future, or maybe they buy the stock because other people are buying it and they hope to make a quick buck. All this activity is disgustingly risky. I wouldn't advise it even for professional money managers, and it's definitely a silly thing to do if you're just a beginning investor. What if earnings never pan out? Then Internet stocks are a house of cards, built on a flimsy foundation and ready to topple at any moment. True investors invest in companies with already profitable operations. The only thing we're betting on is future growth, but that's a lot easier if you've got an economic foundation. Most important, we embrace the idea of a margin of safety.

Margin of Safety: The Oldest Trick in the Book

You're driving on the freeway in icy weather. It's snowing, and you can't see well. Do you drive at the normal speed limit, or do you drive under it? Of course you drive under it. You do so to give yourself a margin of safety, room for error. If traffic slows down suddenly, you don't want to have to slam on the brakes.

Warren Buffett gives another explanation of this concept. He says, "You build a bridge to carry 10,000 pounds, but you only let 5,000 pounds over it at any time." As intelligent investors, we can apply this idea to buying stocks. This isn't a new concept in investing; it was pioneered by Ben Graham, a professor at Columbia University and a successful, wealthy investor himself. He was one of the first value investors, and the granddaddy of the margin of safety concept. He wrote his first major work, *Security Analysis*, in 1934, right after the Great Depression. In the midst of a depression, not too many people want to buy stocks. This gave Graham a whole slew of quality, low-priced companies to choose from.

Margin of safety, when applied to investing, means you don't trust yourself blindly. You know how to evaluate how much a company is worth—the valuation. Let's say you've surveyed the earnings and the company's growth products, and you think that the company is worth $100 million. If the stock has a market capitalization of $103 million, you'd pass it over. But what if the price on the market is $30 million? Then you have a steal. In effect, you're buying a dollar bill for $.30, 100 million times! The less you pay, the higher your return on investment is.

Spotting the Right Time to Buy

The toughest thing to do is to figure out if the low price of a company is a signal of financial sickness or if it's a buying opportunity. In fact, the ability to do that distinguishes an average investor from a great one. I've already told you that the market moves in cycles and that there are periodic buying opportunities. But how do you spot them?

First of all, one of the best times to buy is during a general recession. When we fall into a recession, you'll hear about it. Recessions are an inevitable part of the economy. And, like the economy, they're unpredictable. When the 1973 recession and subsequent bear market hit, Warren Buffett wrote that it was *time to get rich*. That seems like a foolish statement in the midst of a downdraft, but it was prescient. Because stocks were selling at such low prices, he made some of his best investments, buying stakes in companies like GEICO, an insurance company, and several other investments that would yield billions in the future.

A second time to fish for good stocks is in the midst of a recession within an industry. These are much tougher to spot, but you'll find, for example, that the stock prices have moved downward. Sometimes these moves aren't justified. For example, in the summer of 1999, several Wall Street firms suffered sharp declines in their stock price. At the time, the Internet brokerages were picking up steam from the Internet stock hype. These Internet brokerage firms are wonderful companies to invest *with*, but not to invest *in*. Because of the remarkably low commissions they charge, many of them haven't made a profit. However, as the fever of speculation grew around the Internet stocks, these firms saw their stocks double or triple in price in months, while their offline competitors all faced sputtering stock prices.

I spotted opportunity. When I looked closely at the offline competitors, I noticed a number of hidden profit points that didn't justify the low stock prices. For one, even if Internet brokerage firms stole every single account from their non-Internet competitors, the companies not on the Internet would still make a good profit. That's because many of them had other profitable operations—including managing money (asset management, in Wall Street speak) and investment banking. What's more, the Internet brokerages were everywhere. Conceivably, the Internet firms should've been clobbering their competitors. In a perfect world, everybody would use the Internet brokerages. This is the real world. Consequently, some of the offline firms hadn't even suffered lower profits and many had seen consecutive *quarters* with substantial earnings growth.

You may also find opportunities to invest in quality companies that are facing problems that are *clearly* temporary. I emphasize *clearly*, because you'll be able to spot them instantly. It's common for these temporary problems to cause "one-time charges" (they're paid for with profits) or be the result of a mishap. Still, the stock may suffer egregiously because of it. In general, the market is so myopic that these one-time charges offer some of the best opportunities to invest. Perhaps the best example of a one-time charge happened in the mid-1960s. A commodities dealer had borrowed $60 million from American Express, the credit card company that also engages in special financial transactions like loaning money to corporations. When a bank or financial services institution like American Express lends money, they need "collateral," some asset worth as much as their loan that they can take control of if the loan's not paid back. The dealer put up $60 million of salad oil, which American Express accepted. The dealer failed to pay back the loan, and American Express moved in to take control of this salad oil. Lo and behold, they discovered that it didn't exist. American Express was in the hole for $60 million, a lot of money in the mid-60s. While this teaches you that you shouldn't expect to receive repayment in salad oil (besides, is there really $60 million of salad oil in *the entire world?*), it also provides a fundamental lesson in investment.

At the time, the stock dropped severely. Our favorite hero, Warren

Buffett, stepped in to buy American Express stock, investing 40% of the money he managed into the company. It wasn't as heroic as it was intelligent. Buffett reasoned that the mishap was the same as if the company had paid $60 million of profits in dividends but the check got lost in the mail.

Opportunities like this happen all the time. The difficulty is finding them in companies that are otherwise attractive investments. But they do exist. Over a year ago, UPS announced that it had failed to pay millions of dollars in taxes one year in the 1980s. UPS is public now, but it wasn't trading back then. If it were, I'm sure its stock would have tanked. With the market inching to unsustainable levels, these are the only real opportunities out there.

To understand how overvalued the market is, consider the S&P 500. For our purposes, let's say the index is one stock. As of this writing, that stock has a price-to-earnings ratio hovering around 25. In other words, when the S&P 500 is at $1300, earnings are $52 (1300 ÷ 52=25). That means our earnings are 4% of the price of the S&P 500. On top of that, some of these companies issue dividends. Dividends add only about $26 per share to our fictitious S&P 500 stock. In total, earnings and dividends equal $78. If we divide $78 by $1300, we get 6%. Since we consider earnings and dividends a measure of return on stocks, the return on the S&P 500 is less than the current rate of return on an ultra-safe government bond. Corporate bonds, while riskier, are still considerably safer than stocks, and they yield 8%. To be a competitive investment, the S&P 500 and stocks should yield at least 10%. They don't. By all measures, they're overvalued. In light of that, finding stocks selling at attractive prices—even stocks with temporary problems—is virtually impossible. Sure, it's frustrating advising people not to invest when everyone wants to, but it's sensible.

When times are rough, on the other hand, it's intelligent to shop for bargains. You may not have to look for companies suffering momentary blips. Large numbers of companies may be selling at attractive prices. It may take courage to scoop these companies up during rough times, but it's the only way to go. If you invest during high times, you're wishing and hoping either that earnings make massive jumps to keep up with the stock prices or that other people are willing to continue the speculative binge that's bolstering stock prices. Both of those alternatives are iffy, so be intelligent: Don't invest with the rest, invest with the best—when prices are attractive.

Besides that catch phrase, in this chapter we learned . . .

- The gumball machine example. If the gumball machine could make $100 a year for eternity, it would be best to pay $1000 or less, creating a 10% return on investment in the first year.
- When looking at a stock, consider the earnings as your return on investment. Also, be sure to consider what the prospects for growth in the next year are. Thus, if a company earns $1 million this year and has grown at a 25% rate for the past five years, expected earnings should be $1.25 million. Paying $12.5 million for this company (if there were a million shares, that would be $12.50 a share) would give you a 10% return on investment.
- The best time to shop for bargains happens when there's (1) a general recession; (2) an industry recession; or (3) a clearly temporary problem with the company.

A Real-Life Example
(A Little Less Math)

Now that I've bored you beyond belief with numbers, we're actually going to go shopping for a stock. I ended up purchasing the stock—Cisco Systems—at about $27 a share. As of this writing, it's gone up to $130 per share. The price is far too high now and it happened too fast, but consistent with my theory, I always keep great companies. If I owned 100% of Cisco, I wouldn't sell it just because the market pegged some extraordinarily high number on it. But why did I buy it in the first place? Could you do the same? The answer is *certainly*.

I'm going to take you through all the steps that I went through when buying this stock, and you should be able to repeat the process easily.

Not surprisingly, all these steps are in line with the principles I've set in the last two chapters. In the end, Cisco was, at best, a good buy, but it's the most recent example I can give of purchasing a stock. While I didn't leave enough of a margin of safety, I can expect that the company will grow in the future, and that my decision to buy at this price was intelligent.

Step 1. I'm bored one day so I (a) go to a movie, (b) read a magazine, or (c) screen stocks.

The best choice is *definitely* "c." Why would you want to do anything fun? Actually, I wasn't bored, I was looking for some stocks to recommend on my Web site (okay, maybe I was a little bored). I went to www.rapidresearch.com, and I clicked on "Advanced Screening," which allows you to enter several criteria.

The criteria I typed in were: For five-year earnings growth, the stock had to have at least 10%. That means earnings had to grow 10% a year—at least—for the past five years. The return on equity had to be above

15%. The debt/equity ratio couldn't be above 0.3, which means for every $1 of equity, there's only $0.30 of debt (money the company has to pay back to lenders). In the profit margins section, I put in a minimum of 15%. Margins, as you remember, are *very* important. Unfortunately, there's no box for great management or great economics. But the numbers do tell you something about the company.

As I was paging through the companies that came up on the search, I saw Cisco Systems. Instantly I recognized a winner. I use the Internet, and I'm familiar with technology. As you know, I'm a computer nerd who has a Web site, so I understand how the Internet is put together. And one of the key elements is the Cisco Systems router. Cisco has a virtual monopoly in that field. Later I talked to a friend, a guy who understands how computers are networked, and he told me Cisco was the name to trust. I was very excited.

I pulled up the page on Cisco, and the numbers looked wonderful. Profit margins approached 20%. Return on equity was 20%. The company's earnings didn't just grow 10% a year; they doubled them virtually every year. Of course, I knew they couldn't keep up that pace forever, but the high returns on equity meant that as they got bigger, they were still doing excellent business. I figured Cisco could grow earnings at 15% for at least 10 years.

Step 2. Order the annual report.

I ordered the annual report on the Internet. There are several services on the Internet that will send you a company's annual report for free. I prefer www.annualreportservice.com.

In reading the report, I wasn't happy to see that John Chambers, the CEO of Cisco, was a little too slap-happy with the company in the letter to the shareholders. He wrote about its amazing future and its wonderful products. When I was done reading the letter, I believed that Cisco was the most important company in the world and vital to the existence of humankind. I say this, of course, with heavy sarcasm. The one gripe I had with the annual report was Chambers's unrelenting enthusiasm about his company. While some may see that as positive, too much of a good thing shows that something isn't clicking right.

However, I eventually realized that management was doing a fine job in other areas. In my research, I read an article in *Fortune* about the company selling its products on the Internet. Cisco even makes money selling gift items—like Cisco pens—on-line! Still, I never like a CEO who's a salesman. A CEO isn't in his post to justify every shortcoming or to present his company as spotless.

I've never met John Chambers, but I've read enough about him to know that he has an amazing reputation as a businessman. Chambers isn't like most managers of technology companies. Unfortunately, with a lot of these companies, the people who run them are computer geniuses but lack enough management skill to write a to-do list. They're capable of making whole programs themselves or building computers by the dozen, but they can't run a business. To be honest, most of them look and act like computer nerds. Management requires a different skill set. A manager needs to be decisive and in control. Raw intelligence only goes so far.

You'll find some of your gripes can be dealt with. If you don't want to peruse the annual reports yourself, you can order annual report cheat sheets through my Web site for some of the major stocks. However, it's best to do your own reading. In reading Cisco's annual report, I noticed, for example, that their profit margins were falling. Management attributed that to higher sales of certain low-margin products and lower sales of more profitable products. Margins are important, but the company was growing rapidly. Earnings have to be fueled by something. The rapid clip of earnings growth more than made up for the slowly decreasing margins. What's more, I wasn't and still am not convinced that a company that sells half of all the Internet routers in existence will have to cut prices dramatically to defeat competition, like some companies that don't have such a stranglehold on their market.

Next, I found an annoying tidbit in the report involving employee stock options. In order to lure management and employees to companies, the company needs to hang a carrot: stock options. Options are the right to buy stocks at a certain price by some date in the future. We'll discuss options as an investment later, but think of it as stock that you can't have now, but you'll get in the future. Employees don't have to pay for these options; they're a pure, no-strings-attached incentive. With the feeding frenzy of Internet stocks now, potential employees figure that their options could be worth thousands or even millions. Several early employees of Microsoft are now millionaires because of their options. They may be thrilled by their good fortune, but options are a pain.

Somebody needs to pay for them, and the money always comes from the shareholder's pocket. The company issues more shares. For example, the company may issue 490 million stock options, of which almost 200 million are exercisable, meaning they can be turned into real shares and dilute earnings. In fact, if you read an annual report, you'll find two EPS figures: basic and diluted. Diluted includes those options, while basic doesn't. As it happens, Cisco was issuing options that were having an impact on the earnings. While I didn't like it, I could live with it. The company had about three billion shares on the market, and Cisco had set aside 200 million exercisable options.

I found the company outstanding. With several pluses and very few minuses, I was happy. Yet, even with all the great words I have for the company, I wouldn't have bought it if the price was too high. At the time, technology stocks were in a general downturn. But nothing in the industry had changed. Earnings were exploding. People were worried about the prices of the stocks. They thought they were too high, especially for technology. Their fears fulfilled themselves. Stocks dropped enough that there were good bargains. Cisco traded at $40, then $35, then $30. As the price got cheaper, my potential return looked better and better.

CISCO SYSTEMS

Pros	Cons
Profit margins of 20%	Overly optimistic CEO (does he deny any faults with the company?)
Return on equity of 20%	
30%/+ growth of earnings per year	Too many stock options
Management expertise	Margins decreasing somewhat
Good price considering growth	

Why? Earnings were about $0.75 a share. When the stock traded at $25 a share, it was like getting a 3% return—immediately ($0.75 EPS ÷ $25 a share). While that doesn't compare to a good bond, I was banking on growth. Earnings were growing at about an average of 50% a year, but that will slow down to the pace of their return on equity—19%. To me, this was a great deal. It's very similar to a bond in which your interest payments keep getting bigger. Essentially I'm getting a bond that pays 3% the first year, with payments growing at least 19% a year for every year after that.

Don't forget the last test. Does every dollar kept by the company increase the market value by at least a dollar? As it happens, Cisco kept every dime they earned in the last five years. And the stock has gone up several hundred percent. Each dollar retained pushed the stock price up more than *five* dollars. I don't expect that to continue, but if it does, I can expect a very lucrative return on my investment. Actually, I thought of Cisco growing at about 20% annually. That's an excellent return, and I'm definitely pleased if it happens.

However, once in a while, the unexpected happens. My money tripled in three months. Companies with Internet-related operations exploded, and Cisco is up over 500% as of this writing. None of this, however, fazes me. I wouldn't be concerned if Cisco was down 10%, either. I studied the business, I researched it, and I made an intelligent investment decision. If you do the same, I can't assure you triple-digit returns, but I can assure you that, in time, you'll see the market head your way.

Summary: In this chapter, we learned . . .
- How to apply our principles to the real world. The first step is screening stocks in some fashion. This can be done over the Internet or even by glancing at papers like *Investor's Business Daily* that list key financial figures.
- Find companies that fit the criteria we've covered in the last two chapters. Read the annual report. What's management's take on the company? Where are the potential problems? Can they be solved or will they eat away at business?
- Dig deep into the annual report. Read the fine print, including the footnotes. What does management really have to say?
- Always, always, always calculate price. See how much your initial return on investment is, as well as the company's expected growth rate.

Managing and Selling
Your Stocks (No Math)

Before I ever invested a real dime in the stock market, I participated in a contest where, in three months, I made a 12% return on my portfolio. I thought my genius was unparalleled. On top of that, I picked the stocks mostly at random, choosing companies that I knew (*Playboy* and K-Mart were my top performers). When I got down to using real cash, my first picks were sore losers. I experienced the complete opposite feeling—depression—and now this was real money. I was ignorant of how to balance a portfolio with good stocks and stay away from the bad ones. I think I've improved a bit. But I hope that you never have to go through the experience. You can easily learn from my mistakes, and the primary lesson you'll learn is how to manage a **portfolio**, the group of investments you own.

One of the most common questions people ask me is, "How many stocks should I own?" The answer to this is simple: as few as possible. You already know that mutual funds often own a hundred stocks or more, and I think it's silly. Why would mutual funds buy so many stocks? After all, many are run by people with *several* abbreviations like Ph.D. or M.B.A. after their name, and they've been educated at Harvard or Yale. The short answer is that most are trying not to put too many eggs in one basket. They don't want to bet too much on any one stock. And the rules don't permit mutual funds to put more than 5% of their money into any one stock. That means they have to own at least twenty stocks. This is called **diversification**.

Diversification is intelligent only if you're not so intelligent. If you didn't know anything about investing, would you put your money in a few stocks? Or would you put them in many stocks? You'd obviously put your eggs in several baskets. That would balance the good and bad investment decisions you make. Index funds are the best examples of this. Remember them? They often own five hundred or more stocks, and each tries to mirror a certain stock index. With index funds, you won't do any worse than average, but you won't do any better. Index funds are a wonderful investment for the complete fool. You're an educated investor. You demand better than average. By doing your own homework and making a supremely intelligent decision, you can do better than average. That puts you in the ranks of the super-smart investors. And super-smart investors don't invest in five hundred stocks. They buy five or ten.

You shouldn't invest in more than ten stocks. Diversify by buying great companies in several industries. Even though I'm fond of technology, I've recommended everything from financial companies to electric companies. By buying companies in different industries, you'll survive if that industry falls behind. But whether you have five or five hundred stocks, if the overall market goes down, your stocks will go down too. Stocks are like animals moving in packs. Surviving downward movements is important. Trust your decisions. Forget about the price. In investing, the price of the stock is just a scorecard, but what counts is the effort you make in your choices.

For example, I neglected to tell you that after I bought Cisco, the price fell to almost $20 per share, seven dollars below what I bought it at. That would've been a 26% loss if I'd sold. But it didn't faze me. I've learned to survive the shakiness of the market. When you own five or ten stocks, you'll feel that shakiness more than if you owned five hundred stocks. Forget about the business page. Forget about the stock quote. If your parents hassle you about it, explain your investment philosophy. Ask them if they bought a business instead of a stock, would they sell at the first sign of turbulence? Of course they wouldn't, and neither should you. Great businesspeople trust their judgment.

Who shouldn't you trust? You know not to trust the television. But that's not the end. There are several people trying to tell you to buy or sell stocks. Because I run a visible Web site, I always receive mail from people (in reality, just salespeople) about their great investment ideas. They promise to make me incredible returns. I tell them, "Here's what we'll do: Send me your tax returns for the last three years, and if you've done better than I have, I'll buy your investment." (Investment returns have to be reported to the IRS.) And, of course, rarely do they send me a response.

It's not that my record is unmatchable, it's that most people giving you advice have economic incentives behind it. For example, all major firms on Wall Street have "analysts." They write reports about companies, and since it's their job, they have access to all the key people in the company. It *should* follow that they make good recommendations and that the people who follow their recommendations make a lot of money. That's not the case. Analysts have intense pressure to say good things about the company, especially when another division of their Wall Street firm is doing business with that company.

For example, if Merrill Lynch is helping AT&T issue bonds, rarely will a Merrill Lynch analyst say anything bad about AT&T. That's because Merrill Lynch stands to make a lot of money from issuing those bonds. Analysts themselves may not be deceptive, but it's how the system works. Because I understand this, I never follow analyst recommendations.

What's more, most analysts—along with almost everyone on Wall Street—are shortsighted. In their eyes, the most important item in the future is the quarterly earnings report (a.k.a. Q1, Q2, etc.). Quarterly earnings reports include various numbers, such as total revenues, but the most important element is the "bottom line": the profits the company made. If the report fails to meet expectations, people scurry. The stock drops, and analysts decide they want to "downgrade," or lower their rating, of the stock. They may change that as early as the next report. This is a schizophrenic way of looking at stocks—happy one moment, depressed the next. That's why it's best to ignore Wall Street. I don't like people who shift their opinions constantly, and that feeling extends to people involved with investing. I have faith in business, in the economy, and in my ability to pick stocks. So should you.

Only sell if a really excellent opportunity comes around, and the stocks you own don't match up. Such an opportunity may happen during a general recession, when every part of the economy suffers. Even stocks of wonderful companies fall during this period. As you know, the economy moves in cycles. An up cycle is an **expansion**. And a down cycle is—anybody, anybody—a **recession**. Two of the most popular emotions on Wall Street are fear and greed. During a recession, people think the floor is falling from under them and the world is going to end. Yet America has recovered better than any other nation from its recessions.

Some of the biggest periods of expansion happened after painful recessions. There are several examples of this. Between 1981 and 1982, the economy took a breath. After 1982 it exploded, falling again severely in 1990 and 1991 only to come back stronger. Fast-forward to today. The economy is booming, but there's always the potential of the floor falling from under us. The subsequent recession may produce a scary period, but that, too, shall pass. Periods of expansion produce the same frenzy, but with expansion the frenzy is enthusiastic.

Because of the nature of the economy, think of investing as at least a five-year activity. That means you shouldn't sell for *at least* five years. Most people, on the other hand, take the opposite stance. They say, "Oh, I can easily sell this stock when I don't want it, and pick another." Yet only rarely do people sell at the correct times. To trade regularly, you have to have an excellent system—*exactly* when to buy, when to sell, and how many shares to buy and sell.

Instinct tells people to sell when a stock is going up in price. Most people reason that they have a "locked in" profit, so why not sell? In this case, instinct is clearly wrong. Let's assume you own horses. If you own several, you know that one or two will be better than all of the others. These two win all their races, and they're excellent horses. But you wouldn't think of selling just because they've gotten too good. Nor should you sell a stock because it's gone higher in price.

In reality, you shouldn't ever have to sell. Sometimes things will change in your favorite company. They won't be able to grow at 30% a year forever. Their profit margins will go from 50% to 20%. If things are still positive with the company, keep it. Here's a Liebowitz Law to remember:

Own as few stocks as possible and sell only if the company is shrinking (earnings are getting smaller).

You know that being smart about your investment decisions means sticking with a few stocks. Be smart when you sell your stock. You know if the company has gone up in price and you sell, you have to report that gain and give up to a fifth of it to the government. That's not great, so you should sell only when you have to. Sell if the company is shrinking. I'm not talking about earnings that aren't growing fast enough. I'm not talking about losses over one quarter. We're talking at least four quarters of losses. Still, it's a judgment call on your part. In fact, the hardest part of investing is knowing whether a problem plaguing your company is one that will severely damage the company or one that's temporary.

When television began, there were only three networks. If I had been espousing my wisdom back in the day, I would've recommended investing in these networks. For many years, the few television stations in existence had a rich vein of profits streaming in from advertiser money. Forty years later, hundreds of television stations have emerged, eclipsing the three networks. Look at my options today. I can watch ten different news stations. I can even watch a station devoted to reruns of classic sports games or a soap opera channel. Cable television has changed the economics of the business. The three major networks—ABC, NBC, and CBS—are rich, but they're cutting each other's throats for a share of the television market. Investing in the parent companies of those networks wouldn't be as smart as it would've been forty years ago.

Knowing if an industry is threatened is difficult, if not impossible. Of course, it's best to start by never investing in bad industries, even if the world thinks they're wonderful. You know the criteria for investing in a good company within a good industry, and it's wise never to forget those. It's also smart not to invest in industries that face rapid change, unless you understand those companies.

I understand computers, and I know people want value for their dollar. If you recently bought a PC, chances are you didn't pay over $2500. My first computer cost $4000. You can buy a nice used car with that amount of money. Computer prices have dropped faster than people can scoop computers from stores. But that's not a good thing for investors. Remember the rule that we want a company that can raise its price with inflation? That would rule out computer companies. It's almost ironic: Better technology is cheaper than it used to be. That means it's intelligent for a consumer to buy a computer, but it's not sensible to invest in the industry. Because I understand that, I've never invested in or suggested Dell Computer. They sell computers over the Internet and by phone. Because they've bypassed the computer store and sell direct to the buyer, they've been able to cut costs. So buyers are flocking to Dell. They do $18 million a day in sales over the Internet. Yet, as computers get cheaper and cheaper, they become less and less profitable.

To my chagrin, Dell has been the best performing stock of the 1990s. I noticed it in the early 1990s, and I predicted it would fall into troubled times like other computer makers. At the moment, I'm wrong about the success of the company. It's now the number-two computer maker in the world, second to Compaq, but that hasn't changed the essential shortfall of making computers: above all, people are concerned with their pockets. Dell provides wonderful customer service, but ultimately, people are buying from Dell because of the low prices.

One last note. Before you sell, always ask yourself: Will this company be a competitor in ten years? If you can answer yes, then keep the company. Keep it even if the earnings aren't as great as Wall Street expects. Keep it if everybody's screaming, "Sell!" I know the companies I own will be around for many years. They have wonderful products that people need, and they've established themselves in their industries. While they may not grow as rapidly as they have in the past, a safe return of 15% to 25% a year is better than a risky 75% any day.

Summary: In this chapter, we learned . . .
- A portfolio is the group of investments you own, whether that's stock, bonds, currencies, or hog futures.
- The crowd follows the idea of putting your eggs not into a few baskets, but into hundreds. That's the idea of diversification. One of the most popular ways of doing this is through an index fund, a mutual fund that matches the performance of the S&P 500. This is an intelligent method if you know nothing about the stock market. If you want to be above average, don't invest with an index fund.
- It's wise to own no more than ten stocks in varied industries. If you carefully select those stocks, your ability will be rewarded with above-average returns.
- Sell only if the stock you own is shrinking in value—that is, if earnings are in negative territory and aren't expected to recover.

PART III
Other Street Stuff

Banks, Bonds, Mutual Funds, Options, and Futures

You have more than a basic familiarity with stocks. You see how much I like them. But you'll hear of other investments that may look attractive to you. In this chapter, we'll look at a few of them. The truth is, most look deceptively easy; the people who offer them are salesmen, and the only folks getting rich are the ones you give your money to. We'll begin with banks.

The best thing to do with a bank is to keep as much money away from them as possible. Banks are a simple business based on ripping people off: the **interest rate** for borrowing is substantially higher than the interest rate for lending your money to the bank. In other words, if I keep my money in a bank savings account, I'm probably going to get a 3% interest rate. If I borrow money, I have to pay back the bank at 7% interest.

In other words, let's say I deposited $10,000 in a bank account. At the end of the year, I would receive $10,000 plus 3% interest, for a total of $10,300. Another person, Mary, wants to buy a car, so she goes to the bank for a loan. The bank would lend her $10,000 for the car, for one year. By the end of the year, she'd have to pay the $10,000 back plus 7% over that, for a grand total of $10,700. The bank profits by keeping the $400 difference. Banks have millions in deposits and lend millions every year. And they make millions in profits. I think it's a mean joke.

Nobody becomes rich putting their money in a bank. Checking accounts usually don't offer any interest, and savings accounts offer a minimal 2–3%. That barely keeps up with **inflation**. I've skipped over inflation up to this point, but it deserves some mention. Inflation is a general rise in prices. Why is a Big Mac twice as much money as it was fifteen years ago? Inflation. Inflation nibbles away at your money every year. For example, if prices rise 4% every year, in eighteen years prices will double. You can do this calculation easily using the rule of 72. You know that the time it takes for an amount to double is 72 divided by the rate (4%), which ends up being eighteen. In other words, in eighteen years, a Big Mac will be twice as much as today. That may not seem too bad, but consider what happens when prices rise faster. In some poor countries, inflation causes prices to double every three or four years. Imagine that the same car that sells for $20,000 today will cost $40,000 in three years and then $80,000 in six! Investors aren't just looking to outpace inflation, they're looking to lap it several times over.

Another "investment" (banks call them investments, I call them rip-offs) banks offer is a **Certificate of Deposit (CD)**. When I was younger, I thought banks were lending my parents music instead of what they were really doing: offering my parents a higher rate of interest than a normal savings account but forcing many restrictions on them. One of the major restrictions is that you can't withdraw your money for a set period of time. CDs offer various **maturities**. In other words, you can only withdraw money from your investment in a CD after a set period of time without paying some kind of monetary penalty. For example, a CD may have a maturity of three months. If you withdraw your money earlier for whatever reason, the bank may not award as much interest to you. Somehow, they'll find a way to make you pay for taking something they thought was rightfully theirs for three months.

For you, the bank is only a temporary holding place for your money. It isn't a place to make investments, especially when you realize that the bank is making a generous profit by lending the money at a higher rate of interest.

If you do choose to keep some money in a bank, consider Internet banks. These companies don't have to pay for the building, the tellers, or all the other expenses of running a real bank. While the interest you get on your money is pathetic—only 3% on most savings accounts—it's better than most. Don't worry about the interest rate you get at the bank. Since the bank is a short-term stop for your money, don't be overly concerned with how much money you're getting back. If you keep $1,000 in the bank, you'll have $1,030 in the bank at the end of the year.

Instead of worrying about the interest rate, keep an eye out for a monthly charge. I keep a very small amount of money in checking accounts at the bank. I practice what I preach. After I receive a check, I deposit it at the bank, and within days I send that money to my investment account. I learned my lesson when I first opened my account and kept a lot of money in it. I kept my **balance**, or the amount of money in the account, at $1000 for several months. What I noticed, however, was that the money was slowly disappearing. After five months, I had $925 in the account. I discovered that I was being charged a $15-a-month "service charge." It's cheaper to keep the money under the mattress! And I still haven't figured out what kind of "service" I was getting for $15 a month. When I look back at it, I now realize that I was paying almost 15% a year on my money to keep it in the bank. I now keep my money as far away from local banks as possible.

Once I realized the bank wasn't the place to keep my money, I looked at other assets. I first found **bonds**. The easiest way to describe a bond is as an IOU. When a friend asks for money, you're a nice person, so you say, "Here's five dollars. Pay me back as soon as possible." That doesn't fly in the investment world. People are greedy, and that's a good thing, at least for you. Let's use the government, who issues billions of dollars in bonds, as an example. The government says to the average American, "Can we have some money? We'll pay you back in a year and give you some extra money for the privilege of using your money." The government never defaults on their bonds, meaning they always pay them back. It's no credit to them; they can do that because they simply *print* more money. The percentage return on a bond is called the **yield**. Since government bonds are safe, the lower risk also means a lower reward. Between 1995 and September 1999, the yield (also known as the interest rate) has hovered around 6%.

Before we finish our discussion of bonds, let's spend a New York minute on how bonds actually work. Repeat after me: Bond "prices" go up when interest rates go down and vice versa. Let's say you can buy a bond at a 10% interest rate. You "pay" $1,000 for the bond, and you get $100 at the end of the year. No matter what, you get $100 at the end of the year. But let's say the moment you buy the bond, the price of the bond goes to $500 from $1,000. The person who purchases the bond at $500 gets $100 at the end of the year and ends up with a 20% return ($100 ÷ $500) while the person who paid $1,000 ends up only with 10% ($100 ÷ $1000). Don't get bogged down in the details, but remember that *the value of the bond goes in the opposite direction of the yield.*

Another important lesson we'll take out of this is that a stock is like a bond. The "value" of the stock is its price, and the yield is the amount of money it makes—its profits. However, instead of returning a static amount of money, those profits have the potential of going up. So a good stock is like a bond with an ever-increasing yield. And it's best to buy that stock at a lower price, since the yield will be higher.

The government bond is the safest. But if you have a taste for the fast life, you can try a **corporate bond**. Since a bond is a form of credit, there are services that rank the company's ability to pay the money back. The same company that runs the S&P 500, Standard and Poor's, ranks bonds. Moody's Investor Service is another organization that does this. You can check out bond ratings on the Internet. All the bonds are rated "A B C" like grades in courses. Corporate bonds have yields marginally above the treasury bonds, such as 8% or 9%. There are also a series of high-yield bonds called **junk bonds**, with yields in the 14–16% range. They may seem tempting, but they're the riskiest. It's difficult to ensure such high returns, and that's why they're called junk. Donald Trump, for example, has used the money from the sale of these bonds to finance real estate development and casinos. Don't get suckered by the allure of a high return into thinking that this is a good investment. If the bond defaults, you'll get little or no money back.

The one thing that I do like about bonds is that they're good if you have a lot of money already saved. When you retire, for example, let's say you have two million dollars. A corporate bond may yield 8% or 9%, and you may receive close to $200,000 at the end of the year (actually, bonds are paid twice a year—half every six months). What's good about quality corporate bonds (A, AA, and AAA) is that you're lending your money to a large, solvent corporation. Before the company declares a dividend, it has to pay its bondholders. If the company ever went bankrupt, the first people it would have to pay would be—take a wild guess—you, the bondholders!

Unfortunately, a drawback with bonds is that you are taxed on the interest payments as income. That means the government takes a third of your bond income from you. The one exception to this rule is **municipal bonds**. "Muni bonds" are tax-free state or local bonds. When California, for example, wants to finance a bridge or dam, it issues bonds to pay for it. As an incentive to potential investors, the interest on those bonds is tax-free. When you own stocks, unless you sell, you aren't taxed if your stocks go up. You aren't taxed because you have an **unrealized gain**—you haven't sold (made it real).

If you have to pay money to the government every year, as is the case with bonds, you can't take full advantage of compound interest. Say, for example, you have a $10,000 bond. You earn a 10% yield on the bond. That means you make one thousand dollars. The government, in all its generosity, only takes up to a fifth. Let's assume they take the whole fifth. So now you have around $800 to play with. If you reinvest that in your bond, you now have a $10,800 bond. If that bond still yields 10%, you receive $1080. Reinvest that in the bond and it now is worth $11,880. On the other hand, let's say you had $10,000 worth of stock. In the first year that stock goes up 10%. Now, you have what type of gain? Anybody, anybody? Unrealized. Why? Because you didn't sell. You have $11,000 ($1,000 + $10,000). If the stock goes up 10% the second year, you now have $12,100 ($11,000 + $1,100). Compare that to $11,880. While it's only around $200 more, that adds up over time. That's why bonds aren't a long-term choice for the smart investor. New investors take refuge in their safety, but in reality bonds are training wheels for stocks.

After bonds, a common way for new investors to enter the markets is with a **mutual fund**. Let's say your friends decided to pool their money and give it to you, the now-savvy Wall Street wizard. To entice you to manage their money, they offer to give you a percentage of their money. For example, if they hand you $1,000, they offer to give you $10 a week to manage that money. A mutual fund is nothing different. Things just happen on a larger scale. When investors decide to put their money with somebody else, called a **fund manager**, and let him or her make decisions about stock investments, they've invested in a mutual fund. Mutual funds have exploded in popularity. There are more mutual funds than there are stocks on the New York Stock Exchange. That seems to defy logic, but it's the truth. This has happened because people are scared of managing their own money. Entrusting it to somebody else, somebody who appears to be more intelligent than they are about the market, *seems* to be the right way to go. I stress the word *seems*. Most people are wrong. There's nothing that angers me more than seeing investment advisors suggest that people invest in mutual funds.

There are several reasons why you shouldn't invest in mutual funds and only a few exceptions when you should. There are two Liebowitz laws:

(1) Invest in funds only if you have a retirement fund that forces you to invest in them.

Retirement? I'm only seventeen. Right, I didn't forget. But remember the rules of compound interest? Start at age twenty with $2000 at 15% a year and . . . millions are just a couple of decades away. So start a retirement account as early as possible. Your account will probably be in the form of a **401(K)**. I love this type of account. It's tax-deferred, meaning you don't have to pay taxes on your gains until you pull the money out. Recent revisions in the laws make it acceptable to pull the money out for college expenses. You can borrow against the money. That means you can take a loan out against money that you already have.

Things aren't totally rosy. Some employers force you to invest in mutual funds, and there's a limit to how much you can save in any one year. The current law allows $10,500. That's more than the $2,000 a year I mentioned just a moment ago, which is great. Still, some people can afford even more, and I think they should be allowed to add to it.

(2) Invest in funds only at gunpoint.

Okay, nobody will force you at gunpoint to invest. But certain people, called stock brokers, will try to sell you mutual funds. As much as I hate mutuals, they love them. That's because they make money on the transaction when they sell them to you.

From these two exceptions, it should be clear to you that the only time to invest in mutual funds is when circumstances force you to. But there are several other reasons that I'm a passionate opponent of mutual funds.

(1) Eight out of ten mutual funds don't do as well as the S&P 500. Let's say you run track. You know who the best runner on the team is. It definitely could be you, but in my case it's always someone else. Every time you practice or race, you're measuring yourself against that person. If you beat them, you feel pleased. Even if you don't win the race, you're happy to beat this person, right? Of course. The same is true with stocks. The S&P 500 is like the best runner on the team. Fund managers are always comparing their performance to the S&P 500. If this index is down 6% one year and the fund manager made no return,

that manager isn't disappointed. He's only concerned with beating the index.

Even with this obsessive preoccupation, the sad fact is, folks, that 80% of mutual funds don't even do *as well as* the S&P 500.

2) Mutual funds are too big. You're a small investor—you don't have millions of dollars. Mutual funds, on the other hand, are large. Very large. The largest mutual fund, Fidelity Magellan, has $80 billion in assets. That's more than the yearly income of some countries. That size affects their performance dramatically, because it affects their ability to buy and sell stocks.

If you have $10,000, it would be very easy to buy stock with that money. You wouldn't be a big part of trading that day, and it would be pretty easy for someone on the exchange to pair you up with a seller. But imagine if you wanted to buy $100 million worth of stock. That's what mutual funds often have to do. Since they can't buy all they want at once, it makes sense for them to buy "blocks" during the day. With so much demand, the price rises. And the higher the price you pay for a stock, the less of a bargain you're getting. Mutual funds are way too big for their own good, and they're way too big for your own good. Add to that a meager track record, and mutual funds look like bad apples.

(3) Mutual funds have too many stocks, and they buy and sell too much. You'll probably hear the common wisdom (if you haven't already) that it's good to buy and hold mutual funds for long periods of time. This is the worst advice! Mutual fund managers love when people hold money in their funds. They make a percentage of the total assets of the funds, and so they want as much money as possible.

While the fund marketers tell you it's best to hold funds as a long-term investment, fund managers buy and sell stocks at a frenzied pace. Most mutual funds sell 70% of the stocks they buy within the year. For example, if a mutual fund company buys Microsoft in January, there's a 70% chance it will sell that stock by December. In fact, many managers sell it and buy it back again. You've already learned the optimal amount of time to hold investments is years, not months.

Besides turning over their portfolios too often, funds own far too many stocks. I've never seen a millionaire who doesn't specialize. Wealthy people don't get rich by owning a few shares of eighty different companies, like most mutual funds. They focus on five or ten companies, owning large amounts of stock in those companies. The more stocks you own, the less you know about the companies you own. Own as few smart investments as possible. Steer clear of the mutual fund trap.

(4) Mutual funds are expensive! One of the great ironies of mutual funds is that not only do they do worse than the S&P 500, they charge you extra for it. Many times, funds will charge a fee of over 1%—up to 3%—of all the assets in the fund to manage it. For a fund like Magellan, 1% of $80 billion is $800 million a year. I wish my father took home $16 million a week. Of course, that makes sense. You have no choice but to pay the fund manager to do his job—as badly as he may do his job. And you can't shirk his assistant or secretary. You have to make sure that the manager can make the payments on his Ferrari. Sometimes, funds take an extra bonus—a percentage of the profits. That's great if I work for the fund, but not if I want to invest in it.

I find that most people invest in funds out of laziness, not out of careful analysis. Fidelity has a brand name, and it's a mental shortcut to invest in a fund with a good name. It's like buying a stereo. You can go out and look at every stereo on the market, carefully note all the features on each one, and make the most informed decision. Or you can buy a Sony.

I don't hold it against you if you take brand-name shortcuts. But I do have a word of advice: If you're not willing to follow the advice in the rest of this book on choosing companies, *invest in an **index fund***. An index fund is a fund that owns all the stocks in the S&P 500 or some other index, like the Dow. While the index funds don't mirror the movements of the indices exactly, they do a very good job. Index fund managers never buy or sell unless the composition of the S&P 500 changes. And the expenses are often minimal: 0.5% or less. If you really can't commit yourself to learning about business and investment, then these are the right investments for you. I can't tell a fib and say that learning to invest doesn't require some effort. But it ain't the Navy SEALs, people. Index funds are very average, and I think you have to lack confidence in yourself to invest in them. But for many, many people, they are the right choice. And they are certainly better than the average mutual fund.

Money is important. You study in school to get a good job. You get a good job to make money. Money is important. But your confidence is more important. Develop confidence by investing yourself. The time required is almost nothing. You can hold investments over years, add to those investments, and make heaps of money. Or you can let somebody else do it and not have a clue about what's happening to the money you've spent hours making.

Options: A Choice Not Worth Making

Today's investment-of-the-moment is the stock **option**. For the most part, stock options are fraudulent. They aren't an investment, they're the riskiest way of speculating in the stock market. Unless you work for a company that can teach you how to trade options, don't.

The only real reason I've learned about stock options is to understand why companies dole them out by the dozen to potential employees. Stock options are incentives to work for a company. For example, if Cisco Systems thinks I'm a great executive and can make a lot of money for the company, they may offer me options to work there. For example, they may give me 10,000 options if I sign up to work. These options would entitle me to buy stock in the company for $20 per share anytime in the next three years (the three years is an arbitrary amount). At the time I sign the contract, the stock is $20 per share. So my options aren't worth anything just yet. However, if the stock goes to $60 per share in two years, I can exercise my options. I can take 10,000 shares at $20 per share and immediately sell it at $60 per share. That would give me a $400,000 profit! However, if the stock fell to $5 per share before I exercised my options, I could just let them expire—do nothing. While I wouldn't lose any money, I wouldn't make any either. These options can't be sold to someone or traded in any way.

But there are some types of options that can be traded, and these have gained tremendous popularity. What are these options? Basically nothing more than a contract. Call options are buy side options. In other words, you would purchase a call option if you think a stock is going up. Let's say the stock is at $80 per share. So you choose to buy one contract of February 75 calls. Next month is February. Since a contract is 100 shares, the February 75 call gives you the option (hence the term) to buy the stock at $75 per share by the third Friday of the month, the expiration date for every option. Every option has a price tag. I won't go into how options are priced, but it suffices to say that it is very complicated. The other type of option allows you to sell stock by a certain date. It's called a put. Unlike the previous class of options, traders buy and sell these contracts to each other trying to egg out a profit.

A put gives the right, but not the obligation, to sell a stock at a given price by a certain date. Thus, if the stock goes down, you make money. At best, these options are a challenge in mathematics. Most people don't realize that people who buy puts and calls often lose money on their options. Purchasing options is a foolish investment.

Yet, that's where the trend is going. The lure of big bucks is too tempting. I went to a free seminar given by Wade Cook (I wouldn't pay a dime for any of this). He's a big guy in the options game. He's spread the gospel of options through his bestselling books. In reality, his books are just a bunch of marketing hype for his seminars, which go for about $1600 for a couple of days. So I went to this free preview seminar in this nice hotel banquet room, and the leader of the seminar gets up to the lectern and starts talking about options. "You just look at a chart, and here it shows you buy, blah blah blah," all worthless techniques. And then he starts talking about his boss: "So Wade bought here, and sold here, and he made hundreds of thousands of dollars on this account that he started with a few thousand." So I'm sitting there and I can see all these people with wet lips, thinking about what they could do with that *extra hundred thousand* they could make in the market! And I'm thinking, "I know all about the market, and none of these techniques work. And he doesn't even mention the possibility of a loss." So I'm prepared to ask a question, knock him down a notch, and he says, "No questions. We'll have questions in private after the conference." I later learned that Wade Cook lost $800,000 in 1997 trading securities, even though the stock market had a record year.

The moral of the story is *buyer beware*. People love to avoid risk. And they love the idea of easy wealth. Advertise a product that has "no risk," a "money-back guarantee," that's "new" and offers "extraordinary opportunities to generate cash flow" and you have a recipe for success. Study after study shows that simple words or phrases like these are hooks. Don't be a fish. Fish are stupid. People who get rich selling products do just that. They don't get rich using their products.

Futures: They Don't Look So Bright

Futures are similar to options. But instead of being based on stock prices, they're based on commodities. The idea of futures is old, but the institutionalized trading of futures is much younger. A long time ago a farmer would say, "I'm worried about having enough heating oil this winter. I think the price will go up by winter, and the price looks pretty good right now. I wish I could buy some right now and have it delivered in a couple of months." Futures trace back to the Bible, when Joseph interpreted the Pharaoh's dream to mean he should save corn during good times and deliver that corn in the future when times were rougher.

Today futures are traded in contracts, like options. Nobody wants the heating oil anymore, they just want to profit from buying the contract and selling it at a higher price. So people trade futures contracts on many commodities. Futures are highly **leveraged,** meaning that the investor can borrow a lot of money and buy a lot more contracts. In the stock market, if you want to buy 100 shares of a $10 stock, a beginning investor would have to put down the full $1000. In the futures market, if you wanted to buy $10,000 worth of corn, most seasoned futures traders would only have to put down $5,000 or less.

Fortunately, the general public hasn't caught on to futures trading. It's another gambler's game. There are ways to succeed, and since there is so much leverage, people start with small amounts of money and sometimes make millions. But these are a special few, and they aren't investors. This is not their hobby, it's their life.

What's more, when we're talking about these few individuals, understand that they have systems and methods for trading the markets. In reality, about 90% of people who trade futures lose or barely break even. Even the futures supertraders make money on only a handful of trades—that is, buying and then selling at a higher price. They may lose money on several trades. The normal investor would be hard-pressed to deal with ten losses in a row! I passionately believe that what one person can do, another can do. I believe that you can become a successful trader if you choose to work years at the job. No successful trader trades part-time. Trading is their life. Jack Schwager, in his book *The New Market Wizards,* interviews a currency trader who has a currency quote machine in his bathroom (among, of course, several other locations in his house). For most of my readers, investing is a hobby, not life. However, if you have enough commitment, you can be as successful as you choose.

Even though I wouldn't work in futures, I love them anyway. The futures markets are a spectacle. Traders gesture wildly, and each hand signal means something different. If you think the New York Stock Exchange is hectic, visit the Chicago Mercantile Exchange, one of the largest commodities exchanges. From above, it's a mass of color. Each trader has a colored jacket indicating his firm. On the floor, it's an insane, loud, and chaotic catastrophe. Most successful floor traders don't stay on the floor all their life. They "move upstairs," in other words, manage other people's money trading futures *away* from the floor. It's a welcome relief from the pain.

Summary: In this chapter, we learned . . .

- About every bad investment in the book. We talked about banks, which lend you money at a much higher rate than you're allowed to save at.
- Bonds are IOUs. You give money now and hope to receive it later. The risk of the bond goes from government bonds (the safest) to corporate bonds to junk bonds (the riskiest).
- Mutual funds are not worth the time spent learning about them. Not only do most do poorly, fund managers charge you more for the privilege of investing with them. On top of that, they trade up to one hundred stocks daily, but they tell you to keep your money with them for the long term. Pshaw!
- Options are contracts to buy or sell certain stocks at a given price at some future date. Option prices fluctuate so much that there's a potential to lose a lot of money in this field. But hucksters in every direction claim they're a great "investment."
- Futures are options on oil, grain, and other "commodities." A select, immeasurably talented group has become super-rich trading these, but for the new investor not willing to spend years learning their techniques, futures are not an intelligent choice.

12

Bad Ideas on the Street

The last chapter should have proved that stocks are the best invest-ment. But even among stocks, there are a lot of bad ideas. For every way of making money, there are a thousand ways of losing it. As a new investor you're especially prone to these ideas. When I first got started, I didn't know which way to go. I was blown around with the wind. Soon, however, I discovered how the successful investors do it. I learned the information that you've learned and the information you'll pick up in the next few chapters. But before we get there, I want to caution you: Watch out for ideas that don't make sense.

First and perhaps the worst is the idea of an efficient market. This is a term thrown around in academic circles. The scientific name is the **efficient market theorem (EMT)**, and it says that you can't beat the return of the S&P 500 or the Dow, the index funds that aren't touched by human managers. That's because, the theory says, everything that's known about the stock is already reflected in its price. In other words, people who know that Walt Disney Co., for example, will report bad earnings will sell the stock immediately. To see efficient markets, look no further than the dryer situation at the average college dorm: at every given moment, somebody has their clothes in the dryer. There are never any opportunities to get my clothes in the dryer. In the same way, people in the market have figured out how to make money in vir-tually every way—whether using some sophisticated application of chaos theory or standing on the floor and calling out orders. Generally, however, this notion is unrealistic. People know things about stocks, but they don't necessarily act on them. To be fair, many intelligent investment strategists have rehashed this argument and now have varying forms of efficient market theory. I still think they're overly pessimistic about the ability of the average investor to outsmart the market.

Second, if EMT were true, there wouldn't be anybody who beat the market consistently. But there are many excellent investors who beat the market year in and year out. There are many businessmen who achieve higher than average profits. People are beating the averages because of their ability, not their luck. And you're on your way. Embrace the idea that you can do it, too, and you'll never again think like a college professor. Remember: The college professor who claims you can't beat the market lives in a small apartment and drives a hatchback while the people who disagree with him are millionaires and billionaires. Whom do you agree with?

Another group of bad ideas stems from what I call the "risk-free" crowd. We've talked about Wade Cook, the options player. As you remember from the mental beating in the first chapter, risk is part of everything in life. Forget investments. It's part of getting up in the morning—you may have a heart attack and die. Anyone who says there's no risk is a con artist. Charles Givens, the author of *Wealth Without Risk,* was an example of this. Givens's books are still available, with the jackets trumpeting Givens's private jet and gold jewelry, a luxurious lifestyle that most wealthy people don't live. On nearly every page of his book, he writes about "risk-free" investment ideas. One method supposedly offers guaranteed returns of 30%.

There are several other bad ideas you can choose from. Some of the most common advocate short-term trading or the buying and selling of stock. You really can't beat long-term investing. If you trade heavily, you only keep $0.55 or $0.60 for every dollar you earn. The rest goes to commissions and capital gains tax. Thus, there's an inherent disadvantage in trading heavily. However, as commissions have fallen, trading quickly has become even more popular.

CNBC publishes information about the on-line brokerages' "response rates." That means if you go on-line and enter an order, it will take approximately X amount of seconds to go through the system. None of this would matter if people weren't interested in making quick trades—trades so fast that a couple of seconds matter. This is an unfortunate development in the history of Wall Street, and I foresee it eventually fading away when the market takes a dive. For now, however, it's wildfire. I calculated that I receive an average of one E-mail a day asking me if day trading is a good thing. What do you think my response is? "No!" I only recommend day trading if you have a history of working on a trading floor of a real company, like one on Wall Street. Many times these people start their own funds and fail, after several years of experience trading billions of dollars. Imagine what kind of mess the young, naïve, and inexperienced trader can get himself into. Leave the trading to the computers and professionals. I've never seen either one on the Forbes 400 list of the richest Americans. But I've seen plenty of investors who have perfected the art of buying a business. In later chapters, we'll learn the techniques that have made them sickeningly wealthy.

Summary: In this chapter, we learned . . .
- There are many bad ideas to choose from on the Street.
- Academics believe strongly that nobody can beat the market consistently. People beat the market all the time. Don't believe people who wear glasses.
- There are no "risk-free" ways to make money. Making a profit requires energy and effort. Don't believe people who write books about risk-free methods. They make money from selling books, not from their investments.
- Don't trade for the short term (yes, I will say it again). There are no "day traders" on the Forbes 400 list of the 400 wealthiest Americans.

Taxes

Sometimes the hardest part of making money is keeping it. That's definitely true with stocks. Although you may buy and sell a stock for a tidy profit, you won't be able to keep all the money you rake in. A large chunk goes to the government in the form of a capital gains tax. We've talked about taxes before and how much they hurt, but when we dive deeper, we see that although we may not be able to avoid them altogether, we sure can come close.

The IRS: The Ever-So-Pleasant Kiss of Death
We've mentioned in passing the IRS, which I call the kiss of death. The acronym IRS stands for Internal Revenue Service, and it's the government agency responsible for collecting taxes. I can't imagine why anyone would sign up to work there. Personally, I find it difficult to extend any sympathy towards tax collectors.

As you'll figure out quickly enough, taxes aren't the most enjoyable things in the world to pay. When I handle my own money, my goal is to pay zero taxes. That's usually not possible without breaking the law, but I can still dream, right? Even if it is a fantasy, the young investor should learn all he or she can about taxes. That's especially true since they may not be a big problem today, but they will be in the future. And the future's right around the corner: the moment you start working, the government takes a piece. The more you work, the more the government takes. People who make over $200,000 pay an average of 44.5% of their income to the government. That means they work almost half the year for the government. Most of this money is taken in the form of an **income tax**, a tax directly taken from your paycheck. In fact, since the tax laws change very often, you may find that the government actually owes *you* a refund. That's a rather novel idea.

Still, the government is woefully ignorant with that money. They fall victim to Rich Kid's Syndrome. The children of rich parents don't value money because *they don't earn it.* The government hasn't earned the money, they've collected it. And they waste it. If the U.S. government were a corporation, it would be a pathetic investment! It has trillions of dollars of debt, and for several years, the government has spent more than it's received.

What's more, the tax law is so complex everyone desperately needs a good accountant. An accountant does a *personal audit,* meaning he tracks your income and spending and sees where you can save and where you have to pay on taxes. He doesn't have it easy, either. The IRS says all the tax forms take about ten hours to complete, but the average is really closer to twenty-one hours. And people pay from $40 to several thousand dollars for professional help. So not only do you have to work during the year for the government, you also have to work overtime around April 15th, the day taxes are due. If you don't do your taxes properly, or your taxes look overly suspicious, the IRS will *audit* you themselves. An **audit** is an investigation into your taxes, and the average person pays out $5,000 to the IRS after an audit.

If you forget about taxes, you'll face a lot of unnecessary hardship when you start making some real money. You can do something: learn. I suggest you read the current edition of *How to Pay Zero Taxes* by Jeff A. Schnepper. This book explains every way you can lower your tax bill. Focus on the sections that deal with minors. A minor is any person under eighteen, and there are special laws regarding our money. Right now, remember that there are three ways you can get around taxes:

• **Tax exclusions**: This is income that you don't have to report as income. You can make a dollar and actually keep the whole dollar. Many of these are for small items, like meals provided by your employer.

• **Tax deductions**: You can deduct certain expenses from your taxable income. That means that if you make $50,000 and have a deductible expense of $1,000, you can reduce your taxable income to $49,000.

• **Tax Shelters**: These are places where you can invest and you don't have to pay excessive taxes. For example, the IRS wants you to invest in your state government, so the bonds issued by the state called municipal bonds are tax-free. In other words, the income you make from the bond payment isn't considered actual income. It's basically ignored by the government and not taxed. Municipal bonds are also pretty good investments, since they fund low-risk operations like building dams or public schools.

Specifically, there are several ways to lower the amount of money you pay in taxes. As it happens, you're a minor anyway. Taxes are based on the amount of income you make. Each group of incomes is called an **income tax bracket**. For example, if you're a minor and make $10,000, you're in the 15% income tax bracket. So here's a neat trick. Tell your parents to give you their money to invest, even if they want to control how the money is invested. Since each parent (and grandparent, if they wish) can give you a $10,000 gift per year, that $20,000 per year would allow the government to take only 15% of your money away.

Here's an example. Let's say your parents let you pick a stock with their money. You used the principles in this book and less than a year later you have made a $10,000 profit on their behalf. If they are relatively wealthy (make over $100,000 a year), then they have pay up to 30% in taxes for the short-term gain. That adds up to $3,000. But let's say, instead, they give you a gift of $20,000. That's your money, and you invest it wisely. In less than a year, you make a 50% return. You would have to be really lucky, but you do. That's $10,000. This time, though, your income consists only of your parents' gift, so you're in the 15% tax bracket. That means that you only pay $1,500 in taxes, a substantial savings.

Second, by following the principles of long-term investing, you'll minimize any capital gains tax. In other words, if you buy a stock and then sell it eighteen months or later, you pay the least amount of capital gains tax. Selling any earlier means that you'll have to pay more to the government, even up to 30% of your profits, if you're in the higher income bracket. Also, since you are only in the 15% tax bracket if you don't work and your parents give you monetary gifts, then you can pay only 10% on capital gains. Put simply, if you make $1000 profit in buying and selling a stock, you only have to give $100 to the government. While taxes are annoying, paying 10% is better than paying 30%.

Summary: In this chapter, we learned . . .

- The IRS collects taxes on all income you earn. There are ways of reducing your tax burden, like tax exclusions, deductions, and shelters.

- The government takes most of its money through the dreaded income tax. People with incomes over $200,000 a year pay as much as 30% of that to the government.

- You can lower the amount of money you pay to the government by receiving gifts of money. Since this will be your sole source of income (unless you have a job), you'll pay a lower capital gains tax.

How to Get Rich Without Really Trying Hard

We've talked about investing, about how to make money. But how does it all fit in with other money matters? How do the wealthiest four hundred people in America, also known as the Forbes 400 for the magazine that lists them every year, become so wealthy? Before we answer those questions, let's try an exercise.

Imagine yourself as a wealthy person, worth, let's say, seven million dollars. Have you bought the most expensive car out there for the last fifteen years? Are movie stars your neighbors? If you're the average millionaire, the answer is "no"!

How can that be? You've probably seen the millionaire on TV or in the movies driving a Bentley, hobnobbing with other rich and famous people, smoking cigars, and hosting lavish parties at his exclusive home. But the truth is that millionaires get that way by *not* spending. And if you want to have the security of a lifetime of wealth, you'll have to learn to live below what you can afford. This isn't preaching or a bunch of mumbo-jumbo, it's a fact of life. A lot of millionaires don't make a million dollars a year, they sometimes make one-tenth that amount. They build the wealth by not spending.

Becoming a millionaire is no different from training to win an athletic event. Although it's awfully exciting to watch Michael Johnson win the two hundred-meter race in his gold Nike shoes, the race is only a small part of Johnson's work. He had to struggle through workouts, interval training, and weight lifting to become as fit as he is. Millionaires have the same work habits. Knowledge, like the information in this book, can only take you so far. In fact, since everybody's experience is different, you may find that the "rules" in this book really aren't hard and fast "rules"—that you will add your own principles and change some as you progress as an investor.

Still, like anything in life—sports, acting, or business—those who are especially excellent do have a few things in common. I've spent a lot of time and energy analyzing some amazing people who have built up vast fortunes. I do this out of pure greed: I want to join their ranks! And I've noticed that many of them have similar habits. Although each approaches money in a different way, one thing is for sure: the fortunes they created did not appear overnight. You won't become wealthy in an evening, but you will notice that as you adopt these characteristics, your cup will begin to overflow. You may not be able to make practical use of these ideas until later in life, but store them. They'll be invaluable tools when the time comes.

Make these lessons apply to your own life. Our generation spends 75% of the money we earn. Instead of saving, we buy designer clothing and cool gear for our cars. Television advertisers are willing to pay more dollars per person to advertise on a show like *Dawson's Creek,* simply because it's a smart bet that more teenagers will go out and buy their products than will the average middle-aged viewer. This isn't a positive sign. We have some bad habits, but there's a fix: It's between the ears. Think of money as a game. Your goal is to accumulate—not spend—as much of it as possible.

Here are a few secrets of the wealthy. Some of the ideas may surprise you.

1. Wealthy people are cheap, cheap, cheap.

Most wealthy people don't buy fancy cars or palaces. It's ironic that the people who do often aren't that wealthy. They're wasting it on their luxuries. Many people like to keep up appearances.

Ask yourself: Why am I buying this? Sometimes, money consistently flows out of our pockets, and we fail to realize it. I noticed, for example, that I would go out twice a week with my friends for a dinner that would cost me about $10. By eating out only once a week, I ended up saving $520 a year. This prompted me to set a budget for myself. The rich are extraordinary accountants, but I'm just learning. They know where the money flows backwards and forwards. If you're like me, you probably don't know how much you spend going out with friends. Make a note of how much you spend each week. Then look for creative (or not-so-creative) ways to spend less. Maybe you buy video games, for example, when you can rent them cheaply. Or maybe you've saved your money and you want a new car. Is it necessary? If it is, think of other options. Three-year-old cars are substantially cheaper than new ones. Whenever I want to buy something, I think of what Bobby Fischer, a wonderful chess player, says: "If you see a good move, don't make it. There's always a better one." When it comes to buying something, be patient. Something cheaper or more efficient will always come along.

Even extraordinarily rich businesses are used to cutting back. The main office of Berkshire Hathaway, a company that owns many multi-million-dollar organizations, has only twelve employees. Don't start investing or begin a business with dreams of a big house or fancy cars.

2. Wealthy people almost always own their businesses.

Your family is friends with the owner of the neighborhood coin laundry wash. Rumor has it that he's worth several million. How can that be? Like most wealthy people (remember Rule # 1), he drives an unpretentious car and wears inexpensive clothes. So how come he's so rich?

For one, he owns his own business. He works for himself. And if he's worth that much, he probably has several stores. Most people with large amounts of money own their own business. Most of the time the business isn't exotic. The average wealthy guy doesn't have a skyscraper named after him. His name isn't in the papers every day. But he's wildly rich. Unfortunately, your parents or teachers may tell you to forget about owning your own business: work hard and find a good company to work for, they tell you. If you're loyal, your company will be loyal. They'll give you a good retirement plan and essentially take care of you until you die.

That's the worst idea you can have! Today's world has changed. Our parents may like to cling to their old ideas, but you should know the truth. Your parents aren't trying to deceive you. When they were your age, you could work for a company for many years and expect to be promoted for your loyalty and hard work. Today's business climate is far more hostile. You may work for Best Buy or McDonald's for several years and never be promoted. Or you may be hired, promoted, and then rapidly fired as businesses practice "downsizing"—a fancy word for firing people to cut costs.

But the funny thing is, the owners of the business actually become richer when the company downsizes, since they don't have to "waste" so much money on useless workers. When there is no security in a job, I'd rather be the owner than the employee any day. Another Liebowitz Law:

It's always better to be the owner rather than the owned. You can't get really rich working for someone else.

You may say, "But, Jay, this book is about investing. I thought I could get rich doing that." The truth is you can. I'm just educating you about another facet of that: bringing in the income that you will invest.

And the truth is that nobody ever got really rich by saving the income they make from their jobs. I've told you that saving is good. It can make you comfortable, especially if you're saving a good percentage of a high enough income. However, the wealthiest 1% of Americans have about 70% of their net worth in their businesses, and the wealthiest 1% own a third of the nation's wealth. That's indication enough to me that most of them got rich on their own, not working for anybody else.

The reason: Like I said earlier, the wealthy think of money as an investment. If the wealthy own their own businesses, they take the risks of getting started, but they can earn 15%, 20%, or 25% returns on the money they invest in their business. And they get to keep it all (minus some for the government in taxes)! If you work for another person, you may be making a lot of money for your company, but you're not keeping much of the profits.

You may already feel this pain. Say, for example, you work part-time in a clothing store in the mall. You sell $2000 worth of clothing in a weekend. The company you work for makes $800 of profit on that clothing, but you make only $100 working on the weekend no matter how much you sell. It's good to work for someone else for the experience, but your goal should always be to work for yourself. Investing is a way to work for yourself. When you buy the stock of a company, you're considered a part owner, and you're entitled to your share of the profits.

Don't quit your job just yet. Your first jobs are your training ground. They'll teach you about the day-to-day aspects of running a business. The library is your training ground, too. There you'll learn all about being in business for yourself—how to invest your money in yourself. You are the CEO, the Chief Executive Officer, of your own business—You, Inc. You, Inc. is trying to be as happy as possible making as much money as possible with as little work as possible. When you work for someone else, don't be afraid to work for the company that pays the most. Even if your whole idea of work is a summer job, shop around for the one that pays the best.

Another thing that I've noticed about the wealthy is that they often have partners in their business. It's a kind of yin and yang thing. Bill Gates started Microsoft with Paul Allen. Steve Jobs joined Steve Wozniak when Apple Computer (makers of the Macintosh) got started. One partner knocks sense into the other, and both motivate each other. If you ever consider starting your own business, consider a partner. Don't just pick the smartest guy or the toughest gal. Make sure your partner is trustworthy and honest and that he understands business. Otherwise, you might as well go at it alone. Partners (you can have more than one) spread the risk around, and they also help you put many heads together to figure things out. In Chapter 13, we'll talk about how you can structure a business to incorporate two or more people.

3. The wealthy take a good idea and run with it.

Although vague, this is perhaps the most important element of being a business owner. You take an idea that works and you multiply it.

McDonald's created a fantastic moneymaking machine—cheap hamburgers served quickly with (immensely enjoyable) french fries, and then they multiplied it. Ray Kroc, who died several years ago and left billions of dollars to his children, didn't start McDonald's. He bought the hamburger stand about fifty years ago. He then spread his idea. He multiplied it by allowing individual people to buy into McDonald's as a **franchise**. This means that McDonald's allowed a person to pay an up-front fee and a percentage of the profits to the main corporation in order to build and use the McDonald's restaurant, name, and products. McDonald's doesn't give the owner anything except its name and products. The franchisee, as he's called, does all the promotion and runs the business as his own. And since the profit motives of the company and the individual owner of each McDonald's are in lockstep, this operation has been enormously successful. It made Ray Kroc a billionaire and many of the store owners multimillionaires. In fact, the cost of buying a McDonald's franchise is now about $1 million. And there's a large waiting list of people willing to pay it.

Of course, you probably don't have $1 million to shell out for a restaurant. So how do you create and acquire? Maybe you've thought of starting your own business. Start it. I guess I've always had the drive. When I was about five or six, I would sit and sell paper, staples, and glue outside of my front door. Of course, since all this stuff was available in the store unused, only a sympathetic few bought it. After spending some time and energy creating software, I turned to investing. I never realized that I'd be considered a voicebox for young investors, but in my typical, young-capitalist-pig fashion, I've multiplied the idea. I do all kinds of things with the work I love to do and get paid for it, including writing this book. While none of this has made me a billionaire, I've discovered that this principle works well, even if you're dealing with small bananas.

4. The wealthy could stop working and not suffer—if they wanted.

The truly rich have what I call a high **time worth**. You may have heard of **net worth**. It's all your assets minus all your liabilities. But I find that it's a useless indicator. For example, the price of your home is listed as an asset. In reality, however, it isn't an asset. Your home may be worth $1 million, but where are you going to live if you have to sell it? And those monthly payments, called the mortgage, take money out of your pocket, along with the expenses for maintenance and insurance. The home acts more like a liability.

So if net worth doesn't cut it, what does? Time worth. Your time worth is how long you could live if you lost your job. That's a scary thought to many, but it's one you should think of, even though you're young. As you get older, you want to structure your finances so that your job becomes less of a factor in your income. You'll build up money in your investment accounts, and you'll develop businesses that you own but which don't always require your presence.

The idea of time worth is the true idea of financial independence. When I asked you to imagine yourself as a rich person, going to work wasn't part of the exercise. Yet a lot of people who are considered "wealthy" are dependent on a job. They may make wonderful incomes of six or even seven figures (now we say *two* commas), yet they would be devastated if they were suddenly fired. As you get older, work on your time worth. Of course, in our youth, we rarely think about how long we can survive without a job. But as you get older, you may begin to worry about how long you can keep a job. The business world is dynamic and ruthless, and it doesn't play favorites. You are as likely to be downsized as the next man, even if you've been promoted several times. But you can use the times of prosperity to flood your accounts with money and use that money to make more.

Now that you understand the same principles the wealthy understand, I invite you to test yourself. In the box is the millionaire worksheet, a questionnaire I've given to many teenagers. It gets people thinking about money and becoming wealthy and taking risk. For each question, rank yourself from 1 (low) to 10 (high) based on an honest assessment of yourself. Don't lie, nobody's looking. I'll explain the reasoning at the end.

MILLIONAIRE WORKSHEET
- Are you especially ambitious, dedicated, or self-motivated in any one or number of activities?
- If you are able to work, do you?
- Do you like to find ways to use your talents to make extra money?
- Do you like to start things on your own?
- Do you save a lot of the money you make now?
- Are you good at resisting the temptation of buying "impulse" items like designer clothing and accessories?
- Do you consider yourself a leader or a follower?
- Do you have a head for numbers?
- Would you go against the crowd if you felt strongly that they were wrong?

Out of 90, 0-27: Turned off by money and thinking about it; 27-54: Somewhat or moderately interested by money, hazy idea about future; 54-90: Good to strong ideas about money and business.

Don't worry—if you scored in the low range of the survey, you can change! I've known people who were never interested in money and their futures, but when I told them that money wasn't an end in itself, that it didn't require advanced calculus to figure out, and that understanding it meant you could make life infinitely easier in the future, they slowly changed their minds. Carl Icahn went to Princeton and studied philosophy. Ten years out of Princeton, he was a pioneer in corporate finance. People change.

You can probably figure out why I asked you whether you save a lot now, but that's only part of the millionaire equation. Most millionaires have a good head for numbers. They're always thinking about our friend ROI (remember: return on investment) and the profits he brings. Great entrepreneurs are leaders, and they aren't scared to go against the crowd. Many practice what's been called "kaleidoscope thinking." When you look into a kaleidoscope, you notice that everything looks slightly distorted and appears at all kinds of funky angles. Albert Einstein once said, "You can't solve problems with the same thinking that created them." Old Albert applied that idea to physics, and I apply it to any kind of thinking. The super-rich do things differently. They own successful businesses because they did what nobody else did or what everybody else did differently.

Successful people and businesses think creatively. All good ideas sound stupid or impossible. What if you were a businessman in 1980 and somebody told you that a personal computer that looked like a small television set with a keyboard would be on the top of virtually everyone's desk by the year 2000? You would've called them nuts, simply because the idea seemed so silly. Don't be afraid to be creative or go against the crowd.

We've talked a lot about what the wealthy do. How do you apply that to yourself, now? I have three tricks for creating wealth. They aren't magic, because they require some effort, but they work:

(1) Pay yourself first. Always save even before you pay your bills. Put money away before you do anything else. Even though you may not have any bills now, put your money in an investment account before you do anything else with it. I recommend that people start off by saving at least 20% of their income and going up from there. As teenagers, the money we make from a job is called "spending money," but that doesn't have to be spent. I practice what I preach. I put the money I make from my company immediately in the bank, and then much of it is sent to an investment account before I spend the rest on expanding the business.

(2) Buy assets, not liabilities. Never use a credit card, except for purchases for which you can't possibly use cash, like a car. Don't spend

too much money on your car, your home, or other things just for showing off. Nobody likes a show-off. And it isn't any fun to have a luxury car or luxury home when you can't afford it. Have you ever felt the rush of buying something new, like a car or some cool electronic device? I have many times, and unfortunately, I'm still the kid at the candy store in Best Buy. It always seems that once the rush goes away, the toy is no longer as fun as it used to be.

(3) Increase your earnings. If you want to start your own business, start now. If you have an idea for making money, figure it out and quickly execute it. Learn to earn so that you can save and retire early, rather than spend more money. If I earned $500,000 a year, I could become a millionaire relatively quickly without even investing. How? By saving 20% a year—$100,000—every year for ten years. But how could I possibly have an income of $500,000? Most people never will, which is why you have to save and invest religiously. But it's always easier to accumulate when you have more rather than less. The average professional with a graduate degree makes over $100,000 a year. And the median income of a doctor is over $200,000. There are professionals who make up to $1,000,000 a year. Today, specialized degrees are often an important means of advancement. Forty years ago it was almost exotic to hold an MBA, a Masters in Business Administration. Today, some companies require employees to go to business school to get their MBA in order to be promoted. Don't rule out higher education as a way of making money.

Summary: In this chapter, we learned . . .
- The five things the wealthy remember to do: (1) be frugal; (2) own their own businesses; (3) build on their good ideas; (4) increase their time worth; (5) understand compound interest.
- To take the millionaire questionnaire, to see if we already had the skills to be a millionaire. If so, great. If not, we need to practice some mental athletics by training our minds to learn the skills.
- Three ways you can think about wealth *now*: (1) put money away before anything else—pay yourself first; (2) buy good things, like stocks and bonds, with that money; (3) stay in school to make the big bucks in the future.

Starting Your Own Company: It Ain't Easy

Starting a company is a challenge. However, many of the adults I talk to wish that they'd started their own company. Very few who have their own company regret not working for someone else. You don't have to have regrets, and you can avoid regretting your decisions by starting as soon as you can. Don't get me wrong: It's best to be patient until you discover opportunity. That requires preparation, which includes knowledge of the material in this section. You can't start a company if you don't know exactly what a corporation is. Or a business plan.

I encourage you to consider running something small. When people think of business, they think of this big, massive affair with managers and employees. The truth is, businesses can be composed of one person—you. They have many beneficial aspects, including an opportunity to make a small income. Even if you don't have much success, your work can provide a very interesting story and will definitely look good on college applications and your résumé.

I don't say this all as a passive observer, I'm in business! I began five years ago, and now I run a company that distributes several products and maintains one of the most popular financial Web sites on the Net. I'm still nothing compared with corporations that make millions or billions every year. But I do know a little. Even though I'm not super-successful and wasn't even a high-school graduate when I got started, starting my own business helped me make a little money as well as got me into the college I really wanted to attend.

So how do you get started? The first step involves planning. I encourage you to always scope around for business ideas. When I was younger, my father would always talk about ideas for products that he thought would be helpful; he still calls me up today and asks if a certain type of software exists or some such thing. Then look at your strengths. Somebody who is really into talking and communicating could be really good on the phone, selling a product. Whatever that product might be, you could communicate very well. On the other hand, somebody who is more introverted would have difficulty doing that. Make a judgment about your strengths and weaknesses when you consider what you want to do.

Follow that up with a **business plan**. That's essential. A business plan allows you to figure out what's good and bad about a company that you want to start. It includes a statement of purpose, as well as an analysis of how much revenue and profit the company expects. If you have neither, it may seem premature to do an analysis. However, you can almost always hammer out a poor financial idea by spotting potential financial weakness. Yes, an automatic nose-hair clipper is a great idea (not!), but how many are you really going to sell? More than anything else, it knocks some sense into you. You may get bubbly over an idea and go through all the measures of starting the business without even thinking about what you're getting into.

Learn to write a business plan. Not only will it smooth the edges of your idea, it's necessary to attract other people to lend you money— like banks or investors. Without a business plan, you're just another fool with an idea.

One common question people ask is, "Where should I look for ideas?" First, start the business in an industry that you know about. I don't run a trucking company because I've never driven a truck, much less thought about owning one. Bill Gates was an amateur programmer before he started Microsoft, and Steve Jobs and Steve Wozniak, the founders of Apple Computer, built the first Apples in their garage before they moved into a multimillion-dollar facility in California. If you find the idea of starting your own company this early paralyzing, forget it. You can gain a lot of experience by working for somebody else, then make the decision to go work for yourself. Case in point: Michael Bloomberg was a star trader at Salomon. He was fired from the company and ended up starting Bloomberg Financial Services, which supplies accurate, up-to-date information to investment banks. Of course, since he was grounded in securities trading, he knew precisely what his former employers and peers would want. Consequently, Bloomberg is worth several billion dollars.

Sometimes, people work for another company and they get an idea that burns a hole in their head to make the company better. If and when you do get an idea, be your first customer. Ask yourself, "Am I willing to pay for this?"

For example, I was paging through the J. Peterman catalog one day, and I saw several exotic items that nobody in his right mind would pay for. There was even a lighthouse for sale. Later, I learned that J. Peterman had to sell off their whole company at a bankruptcy liquidation because they were going under. They didn't have enough revenue to support the company. Their eyes were bigger than their brain. While there may be about five people in the world who need your product, don't count on them to buy it. Ask yourself, "Would the average person involved in this field need the product?" If the answer is yes, you're on to something.

Once you find a product or service that you *think* people need, survey them. When I began selling guides to companies, I started by asking my friends if they would buy a guide to individual public companies written for young investors by young investors. Many of them were hooked on the idea. Then I asked them what they would pay. By soaking up knowledge, I set a price on the guide that made it appealing. Then I did a little business planning. Because I wasn't betting big bucks or launching a big product, I figured out how much it would cost me to print the manuals and if each copy would be profitable without writing a formal business plan. Either way—a business plan or a scrawl on the back of a napkin—make sure you aren't selling an unprofitable product. If you sell a newsletter for $1.50 a copy and it costs $2.00 to make, you're only hurting yourself. The more popular the newsletter gets, the more money you'll lose.

Eventually, I included advertising in the calculation, under the assumption that I'd sell very little, and I came up with a bright picture. I stayed conservative, gave myself a margin of safety (remember that term), and I ended up okay. In the meantime, I knew that I had a group of teenagers who were interested in learning this material and that the number of people wanting to see an honest, interesting guide would only grow.

	Pros	Cons
Proprietorship	Easy to set up Simple decision making Profits taxed as income	Owner's entire wealth at risk
Partnership	Easier to set up than corporation Profits taxed only once Can survive withdrawal of partner	Owners' wealth at risk
Corporation	Owners have limited liability Professional management	Complex management structure Profits taxed twice

After you've crunched the numbers and you're ready to move ahead, you have several things to decide. Do you want to incorporate? Or do you want to have a partnership? What's a partnership or a corporation? A normal company is called a **sole proprietorship**, meaning that you're the only person responsible for the business. This is the basic business. You start out by going to a place that allows you to file a **fictitious business name**. I never figured out what was so fictitious about it, but it's the title of your business.

After that, you have to file taxes, and the profit you make from the company is reported in your own taxes. Say, however, someone decides to sue you, which isn't impossible in today's world. The judge forces you to pay $1 million in damages to the other party. In a sole proprietorship, they can take away your home and your car. However, there is an answer to this. There's something called a **corporation**. Corporations are identified by Corp. or Inc. after their name. Corporations require a lot of paperwork, and there a lot of laws governing them that I won't explain here. But the gist of a corporation is that if you get sued, your business may go bankrupt, but the government won't collect your personal assets, like your home or car.

Another common form of business is a **partnership**. A partnership is composed of two or more people who share in the profits of the company. The added benefit of the partnership is that you can take on partners who invest cash in your business. One of the best examples of this is the exclusive world of **hedge funds**. In the investment world, there are a number of "elite" mutual funds called hedge funds. Hedge funds are structured as limited partnerships. This means that they are limited to only ninety-nine partners. In this case, the partners are the actual investors in the fund. Often there are only twenty or thirty investors, but those investors invest $15 or $20 million. Since hedge funds are partnerships and not legally mutual funds, they are not bound by the restrictive rules of mutual funds and can invest in virtually any type of security. Unfortunately, partnerships suffer the same fate as proprietorships, since the owners are personally liable if the company is sued.

That's why larger companies will always incorporate. Corporations have some other perks, too. They pay fewer taxes on the first $75,000 of their income. What's more, there are a lot of expenses that can be deducted by the corporation. In fact, this is a shady area, since many corporations deduct so many expenses that they pay very little in the way of taxes. The drawbacks to the corporation involve the need to file a separate tax return and to pay a fee to the government to incorporate. And there are also some laws you have to follow, like the requirement that the owners meet yearly. If you get big enough, you need to incorporate. It's a fact of life.

Unfortunately, a major negative of corporations is their complexity. Law requires corporations to have directors who meet on a regular basis. Also, profits are taxed twice. Corporations actually have to pay a corporate income tax, and then the profits that the owners take are taxed as income as well. For example, if a corporation makes $1 million, the corporate tax will take roughly $300,000. Of the remaining $700,000, let's say the owner takes home $200,000. He'll have to pay income tax on that, which figures to be about $90,000, considering that he's in the highest income-tax bracket. That's an unfortunate fact of life, but corporations are usually so big that there are no other options. Partnerships and proprietorships can't contain a multinational company with hundreds or thousands of employees.

Summary: In this chapter, we learned . . .
- Starting a business is a difficult thing to do. Make sure you understand the market for your product. Moreover, consider writing a business plan or some type of analysis of your business ideas. Sometimes fancy ideas aren't as sophisticated as they sound if they can't earn a profit.
- Your options for structuring a business include: a sole proprietorship, a partnership, or a corporation.

Where to Learn More

My maze of learning was complex, and one motivation I had for writing this book was reducing that to the most important elements. I've read over seventy-five books on money, many of them devoted to investing in the stock market. Many of them have been so complex I've walked away from them dazed and confused. One book, for example, covered *optimal f* and other statistical applications as they applied to trading. And others have been foolishly simple. These books claim magical returns, and whet your appetite with the possibility of turning a little money into millions. Of course, these are false notions. Whenever I've read widely on a subject, I've usually discovered that all the writers approach some sort of consensus. Ultimately, all the books on a particular subject had the same message. With investing, that's the farthest thing from the truth!

Some of the books that I mention may differ from what you're seeing here. Don't fret. However, before you adopt any methodology, remember to ask yourself: Is what I'm reading here sensible? What about taxes? How safe is this methodology? Bull markets inspire all kinds of crazy systems, and many of them can succeed during an up market. However, consider each one carefully. You'll find many are wrapped in salesmanship. Proponents of day trading, for example, may offer you the world, telling you that day trading is a safe, consistent way to churn out profits every day. Rarely do they mention what could go wrong or the full risk of day trading—including the consequences of taxes, stress, and isolation.

In the next few sections, I'll highlight a number of books. Parts of each book may be review, and other parts may be new to you. My goal in providing this information is to ease your path to knowledge, isolating the books that will be most useful to you and avoiding those that won't impact your learning. Each book has influenced my work in some way, and in reading them, you'll no doubt think, "I've seen that somewhere."

Getting Started

If you need a review of the basic material in this book, I suggest you read *Charles Schwab's Guide to Financial Independence: Simple Solutions for Busy People*. While Schwab is a supremely intelligent businessman, his investing advice is simple and readable. I enjoyed his descriptions of how the financial markets work.

In the chapter about information sources, we talked about newspapers. They provide a wellspring of knowledge because they cover more than the television news. And they offer more than magazines, which only arrive once a month, whereas newspapers arrive daily. As part of the subscription, you may receive the guide to reading their newspaper. But *The Wall Street Journal* publishes that guide for the general public, and it's available at your library or bookstore. It's *The Wall Street Journal Guide to Understanding Money and Investing* by Kenneth M. Morris and others. Not only is it an introduction to the newspaper, it's an introduction to investing in general and another volume to brush up on your knowledge of how the markets work.

Another excellent book is *Buffettology: The Previously Unexplained Techniques That Have Made Warren Buffett the World's Most Famous Investor*, by Mary Buffett and David Clark. It isn't a coincidence that the author shares the last name of the subject of the book—Warren Buffett. She's Buffett's daughter-in-law. I've read every book about Warren Buffett (honestly, I have) and this is the best one I've found about his techniques, hands down. Sure, if you'd like to read anecdotes about Buffett, read Roger Lowenstein's *Buffett: The Making of an American Capitalist*, which is a massive volume about his life. But the real core of Buffett's success is how it can be applied to *your investing*. In this book, Mary Buffett explains all of Warren's nine criteria for investing in a company, as well as the (relatively) simple math he uses to analyze a company. If anything, this book is oversimplified, but it's still an excellent read.

As you know by now, Buffett is the world's second-richest man and an investment billionaire. He's the most successful investor I know of, and so I've always had the urge to figure out what makes him tick. Two other fine works about him are *The Warren Buffett Way* and *The Warren Buffett Portfolio*, both by Robert G. Hagstrom, who runs a mutual fund that imitates the Buffett investing style. You'll find that Hagstrom's books are an intellectual step up from *Buffettology*, but tackle them if you can. The second book deals more heavily with when to sell and how many stocks to own. Hagstrom, like me, believes in owning a few stocks among several industries, and he has the studies to prove it.

Long-Term Investing

Now here's what I really like. Long-term investing is true investing. It's not speculating, since you're not risking your money on companies with nothing material to offer. Investing is putting your money into something real, a company that actually earns money but may be in a temporary slump. One book that eloquently argues for this is *Stocks for the Long Run: The Definitive Guide to Financial Market Returns and Long-Term Investment Strategies* by Jeremy J. Siegel. This is a readable work written by an academic who is a professor at the Wharton School. Another academic but understandable book is *A Random Walk Down Wall Street* by Burton G. Malkiel. Both gentlemen are rather nerdy fellows up to their knees in statistics and data, although both books are surprisingly readable. Unfortunately, they both are proponents of the Efficient Markets Theorem. In essence, they believe that the best return a person can achieve year in and year out is equal to that of the general stock market. Thus, they are both advocates of index funds. As you know, I disagree completely, but I think reading their books would be a good education. You may even convert and have success with index funds, which is just fine. There are many paths to high returns in the market.

Lastly, some of the finest investment literature is written by Peter Lynch. Peter Lynch is a person with a track record. He grew the Fidelity Magellan Fund from a relative nothing to the biggest fund in the country, with some $80 billion in assets. His books include *One Up on Wall Street: Using What You Already Know to Make Money in the Market* and *Beating the Street*. What's uncanny about Lynch is that even as a mutual fund manager for several years, he doesn't advocate investing in mutual funds. He's a staunch proponent of investing yourself. I agree. People tend to believe that if they know nothing about the stock market, their best bet is to invest in mutual funds. But mutual funds invest directly in the stock market, begging the question: Isn't it just as ignorant to invest indirectly in the stock market through mutual funds as it is to invest directly? Sure! If you don't know anything about the stock market, the best bet is to hold off investing and educate yourself.

Day Trading and Short-Term Speculating

Day trading is the hottest thing to hit finance since the cheap commission. Whole rooms are filled with people who day trade. Most are unsuccessful, but a lucky few are wildly successful. The current bible for day trading is *How to Get Started in Electronic Day Trading: Everything You Need to Know to Play Wall Street's Hottest Game* by David Nassar. Most day traders think that their access to technology will give them the edge they need to play this "game," but the truth is that everyone has that technology now. These books that are churned out so rapidly often focus on the technology as the key element in the day trader's arsenal. Intellect, and most of all, luck, separate day traders from other investors.

Most day trading books offer the same advice: how to gamble on NASDAQ stocks, which are usually rapidly-moving technology companies. These stocks can move five or six points in several minutes. Most day traders, however, aren't skilled enough to play these stocks. Essentially, they're gamblers. One of the smartest books I've read about day trading is Christopher Farrell's *Day Trade On-line*. He contradicts the idea that trading must be gambling.

Farrell acts like the specialist for a small number of ignored NYSE stocks. I liked his methodology so much, I woke up one morning to try it, and I discovered many hundreds of other people had the same idea as me. Unfortunately, in this bull market, I've found that so many people are hungry to make loads of money that every good idea has been thought of and executed and almost every good stock has been found and exploited.

In between day traders and long-term investors is a different breed of speculator. Many people who trade commodities buy and hold for short periods of time, like three months. In the 1970s, before half of the people in the country had money invested in the stock market, the stock and commodities markets were unknowns. Commodity prices would move in one direction—up or down—for months at a time. During this period, a type of trading called *trend trading* was born. It's as simple as it sounds. You buy and hold when the trend is up, and sell when the trend starts to go in the opposite direction. Today, success isn't that simple. Commodities, especially, are volatile. Gold may go from $200 an ounce to $800 an ounce back to $200 an ounce, all in several months. Long-term trends aren't as visible because more people are involved. William O'Neil, founder of *Investor's Business Daily,* developed a system for investing that's a version of trend trading with stocks. His book is called *How to Make Money in Stocks: A Winning System in Good Times or Bad.* You can't find a more appealing title for a book, but O'Neil's book is out of date. Trend trading isn't possible in stocks, and even if it were, it would still be a struggle for the new investor to learn the techniques.

Today, a more common way of speculating in the markets involves **system trading.** Computers have made amazing amounts of data available at little cost. Professionals and even some amateurs can access this data and test various systems. Systems are based on some idea—like trend trading—and involve specific buy and sell signals, as well as signals indicating how much to buy. A common buy signal might be when a stock or commodity hits a forty-day high, meaning that it hits the highest price of the past forty days.

Some systems employ **technical analysis**, which isn't as sophisticated as it sounds. Technical analysis takes its cues from patterns in the charts of stock prices. This type of analysis is a purely subjective way of looking at stocks. Most people don't need a chart to figure out that stocks are moving higher. Despite this, technical analysis has built a large fan base, and several books are available that mention or make use of it, including O'Neil's work. However, the finest book dealing with speculating, whatever type of system one chooses to use, is *Trade Your Way to Financial Freedom* by Van K. Tharp. After reading several books in the library and never buying any financial titles, I purchased Tharp's book on a whim, and I was blown away.

I suggest you read the book, but beware of how simple Tharp makes trading sound. There are certainly success stories, but since you aren't professionally managing money, spending hours every day on your investments can be nerve-wracking. If you want to read about some of the finest money managers, read Jack Schwager's two superb books: *Market Wizards: Interviews with Top Traders* and *The New Market Wizards.* Both books are written in a question-and-answer format, which I find much better than straight text, which tends to drag. Schwager's background is in commodity trading, so he's biased toward that end of the field.

In reading these books, you'll also find that there isn't anything you can really sink your teeth into. Most of the people Schwager interviews are extremely secretive about their methods. I walked away from the books thinking that each person woke up one morning and became a great trader. However, his books are useful by revealing the stresses of the job. Some of these individuals make and lose millions daily. In fact, I knew this was a serious game when one individual equated his experience in Vietnam with his experience trading. If you need to be G.I. Joe to trade, I don't think it's a stress most young investors can handle!

Options, Bonds, Futures, and More

I haven't dealt much with these subjects because I'm afraid I'll get you on the wrong investing track. However, feel free to read about them. They all fall into the realm of speculation: investing in financial instruments where there aren't any assets to support them. Stock investors are part owners of a company that has assets, and those assets (we hope) produce earnings, which support the price of the stock. This is an illusion at best, because the stock can go anywhere it wants. In general, however, most stocks are a mirror image of the company in the long run. Futures, on the other hand, have no financial assets to back them up. They're *pure* speculation. I stress *pure* because even with stocks you can speculate, but with futures you can't do anything else.

One of the best books on futures is *Greed Is Good: The Capitalist's Guide to Investing* by Jonathan Hoenig, a twenty-three-year-old phenom from Chicago. While the whole book isn't about futures, a good seventy pages is devoted to "speculating." Jon happens to be heavily involved as a floor trader in agricultural futures, so he's knowledgeable about the subject. He goes far more deeply into it than I'd ever venture, in large part because of his greater knowledge base. I also like his book because it's catchy. It's enjoyable to page through and look at all the interesting pictures. In fact, it's meant for the under-thirty crowd, so most readers should slip right into it.

To continue on the speculating path, I suggest you read a book called *Liar's Poker: Rising through the Wreckage of Wall Street* by Michael Lewis. This is the story of Lewis's rise from a Princeton art history major to a highfalutin bond trader at Solomon Brothers, when Solomon Brothers traders referred to themselves as "Masters of the Universe." Besides reading like a John Grisham suspense novel, the book will give you a cheap education on how bonds work without paging through a five-hundred page business school textbook.

On that same reading level is *Den of Thieves* by James Stewart, all about the insider trading scandal that rocked Wall Street in the 1980s. At the time, Ivan Boesky was charged with illegally bribing people and gaining access to inside information to find out the inside skinny on companies.

If you've ever considered a career on Wall Street, consider reading *Riding the Bull: My Year in the Madness at Merrill Lynch* by Paul Stiles. Urban legends have it that people who work on Wall Street are rich and sexy. Stiles slashes through this myth. While straight-out-of-business-school associates may make up to $150,000 in salary and bonuses, the world of the Street isn't as kind as it appears. You'll discover that most of Wall Street is utter chaos, focused purely on anticipating and responding to other people's moves. There's organizational infighting and a host of other problems to contend with. If you've ever considered working for a major Wall Street powerhouse like Merrill Lynch, this may change your mind.

Glossary

Okay, so you don't remember *everything* in this book. That's fine. Use this glossary when this book, or any other one, gets too confusing. If the term you're looking for isn't in here, there's always the Internet or a real dictionary (God forbid!).

401(K): When you finally get off the couch and start working, your employer may give you one of these retirement accounts. The funky name comes from its location in the tax code, but this type of account isn't short of benefits. They include tax-free transactions until the money is withdrawn and, often, matching contributions from your employer up to $9500 per year.

Acquisition: The purchase of a company. Usually this refers to a larger company purchasing a fairly small one.

Annual Report: All public companies are legally required to disclose financial information. Each year, companies produce an annual report that summarizes this information for the year and sometimes includes very enlightening commentary from management.

Ask Price: The lowest price any seller on a market is willing to sell his shares for. For example, if the ask price on a stock is 65, it means there are probably scores of people who would like to sell their stock at 65 $\frac{1}{4}$ or 65 $\frac{1}{2}$, but the lowest price a seller is willing to sell at, 65, is considered the ask price.

Assets: Anything a company or person owns that generates money. If my blast furnace helps me smelt steel, a profitable product for me, then that furnace is an asset. But humans can be assets, too, since they're capable of creating or selling products that generate profits.

Audit: Any examination of financial records. When done by the IRS, the audited person often has to pay to the government. When done by your accountant, it can help you sort out where your money is going.

Even the regular teenager can do a personal audit, if he can remember where all his money went in the last year!

Balance (Checking Account): The amount of money available for withdrawal from a checking account at a bank.

Balance Sheet: A listing of assets in one column and liabilities in the other.

Bearish: A negative feeling about a market.

Bid Price: The highest price someone is willing to pay to purchase shares of stock. It's always lower than the ask price. For example, if the bid is 50 ¾, it means there may be people who'd like to buy at a lower price—50 ½, for example—but the highest price somebody is willing to pay, which is always listed, is 50 ¾. Also called "the offer"—as in, "make him an offer he can't refuse."

Blocks: Large numbers of shares. My mutual fund may want to buy 50,000 shares of a company. Instead of putting an order on the stock market for 50,000, which may never be filled or filled at a very high price, the fund would arrange to trade with people owning smaller blocks, like 10,000 shares, and piece together 50,000 shares while totally bypassing the exchange.

Blue Chip: Large, well-established companies. All of the stocks on the Dow are considered blue chips. The term actually comes from casino gambling, in which the chips worth the most money are blue.

Bond: An IOU. You lend your money to the government or a corporation, who promises to pay you back plus a certain amount, called *the yield*.

Bullish: A positive feeling about a financial market. The stock market, for example, has been in an upward swing for nearly seven years, so the feeling on the Street is "bullish."

Business Plan: A financial and product analysis of a company that hasn't been formed yet. These plans tend to weed out bad ideas by forcing the creator to figure out if the product will sell and where it can be improved.

Buy to Cover: After *selling short*, an individual needs to purchase back the shares on the market. When "covering a short," the person needs to put up real money.

Capital Gains Tax: A tax on gains from investments. The tax is much less if the stock has been held at least a year.

Certificate of Deposit (CD): A bond from a bank, but the "maturity" tends to be much shorter. A CD matures when you get your money back plus your interest. CD maturities range from one month to five years. The longer you lend your money for, the higher the rate of interest. CDs aren't investments, but short-term stopovers for money.

Commission: When you buy or sell stock, a broker takes a piece of the action. That could be from $5 per trade to several hundred dollars, depending on which brokerage you choose. The brokerages that offer "full service," meaning complete access to humans, often charge the most money.

Compound Interest: "The secret of the wealthy." This is the idea that money doesn't just add up, it compounds geometrically. In other words, when you begin investing, your money builds slowly, but as the years progress, not only the principal, but the interest earns interest. The total amount of money earned from investing increases rapidly.

Corporate Bond: A bond that corporations offer to the general public. Most corporate bonds are rated with the A through D grading system, based on how financially secure the company is and its ability to pay back the bonds plus interest.

Corporate Raider: An individual takeover entrepreneur. This was a very chic thing in the 1980s. Few exist today. Raiders, without the consent of the company they attacked, bought up shares in a company hoping to either have their shares bought back by the company for a profit or see the company sell off assets. Well-known raiders have included T. Boone Pickens (oil companies) and Carl Icahn (everything).

Corporation: A company in which the owners aren't *personally liable* if problems arise. In other words, should the company fall into bankruptcy, nobody could take the owners' cars or homes.

Custodial Account: An account created at a brokerage for a minor, a person under eighteen, that is overseen by an adult custodian. While the minor has restricted control over the account, he or she can perform most of the same types of trades as an adult investor can.

Day's Range: The difference between the highest price a stock trades at for the day and the lowest price for the day.

Debt: Also known as **leverage**. Debt is the use of other people's money. Companies incur debt when they issue bonds, and people incur debt when they use credit cards to pay for things.

Delayed Quote: A price quote that isn't up to date. Usually the delay is about twenty minutes.

Delisted: A company is delisted when its stock is taken off the market. All exchanges have certain rules about when a company must be delisted. For example, a stock must fall below a certain price and have fewer than a certain number of shares traded daily before it's finally taken off.

Diversification: The prevailing belief (which I think is dead wrong) that investors should spread their investments among multiple investments. For example, a well-diversified portfolio might include an S&P 500 index fund, since the five hundred stocks in that fund represent companies from all walks of business.

Dividend: When a public company decides to pay a portion of profits to stockholders, it's dividend time. Not all companies pay dividends and not all profits are paid out. Some companies "retain" all their earnings, or only pay out a certain percentage to stockholders.

Dow Jones Industrial Average (DJIA): An index of thirty large, reputable companies. All the stocks are *blue chips*, large capitalization stocks that span across several industries. Intel and Microsoft have been added recently, Goodyear has been dropped. Other notable Dow companies include McDonald's, Caterpillar, and DuPont.

Earnings per Share (EPS): The total profits of a company divided by the number of shares. For a company with $100 million earnings and 100 million shares, earnings are a dollar per share ($100 million ÷ 100 million shares).

Economics: No, this isn't the most boring subject in high school, at least in our definition. Economics refers to the financial nature of an industry or company. A company with good economics, for example, has excellent profit margins and a competitive product.

Efficient Market Theorem (EMT): The (mistaken, I believe) theory that the stock market is "efficient," meaning whatever is known about a stock is already reflected in the price. In reality, as more people enter the stock market, it becomes more efficient, but there are still periods of irrational exuberance or fear.

Emerging Markets: Countries in the world that are earmarked for growth, but currently aren't as developed as the United States. Investments in companies in these countries run the risk of suffering because of political turmoil or a financial meltdown, such as the crisis that plagued Asia in 1996.

Equities: Stocks. Stocks represent equity or ownership in a company, while bonds are a debt that the company bears.

Equity: Assets minus liabilities. Equity usually refers to the "net worth" of a company. If assets are large, for example, and debt is low, the company has a large amount of equity.

Ex-Dividend Date: The latest date you could have owned a stock to receive its dividend. For example, if a stock pays its dividend in March and the ex-dividend date is January 15, you need to have purchased the stock on January 15 or earlier to receive the dividend.

Expansion: An economic period of good health and cheer. Expansions are the up part of the business cycle's ebb and flow.

Extended Quote: A price quote with a ton of information. These are available on-line, and they often include everything from the company's price to its most current return-on-equity figure.

Fictitious Business Name: When registering a business, the name of the company is registered as a "fictitious business name." There's nothing phony about this process. If you own a real business and you want to name it, you have to get one of these.

Financing: The money that needs to be raised for a purpose. We have referred to financing as the money that needs to be raised for a company to go public.

Fiscal Year: The twelve-month period that a company uses for accounting purposes, but does not necessarily begin on January 1. For example, if a company's fiscal year begins in March, it reports first quarter earnings in May.

Floor Trader: If you have a membership on a stock exchange (except for NASDAQ and other small electronic systems, which have no floor) or work for a firm that does, you can go onto the floor and buy and sell stocks. If you ever have the chance to see the NYSE, watch all the people in colored vests scurrying around. Those are the floor traders.

Franchise: A type of company in which an individual pays a company for the right to use its products and name. Several owners of Shell and McDonald's franchises are multimillionaires. It goes to show how powerful the name recognition of those products is.

Fund Manager: The person in charge of running a mutual fund.

Futures: This is a contract for the purchase of something at a future date. For example, if you were a farmer and thought that the price of heating oil would rise in the next three months but you didn't need any heating oil now, you'd buy a futures contract for delivery at the end of three months. Most people who trade futures aren't farmers, but sophisticated investors. There are now futures products for everything from commodities like heating oil to interest rates to stock indices. The casino never closes.

Go Public: The process of selling shares or ownership in a company to the public. Companies go public by raising money and interest from investors. They employ the help of investment banks like Goldman, Sachs, & Co.

Hedge Funds: A fund allowed to use aggressive strategies not available to mutual funds. By law, a hedge fund is limited to under 100 investors, so the typical minimum investment is $1 million.

Income Statement: A financial sheet of figures that shows all the inflows and outflows of money. Inflows are considered income, and outflows are expenses. What's left over is the profit.

Income Tax Bracket: The proportion of income an individual must pay for federal, state, and/or local income taxes. A 20% income tax bracket would imply that a person would have to pay 20% of their income in taxes. The income tax brackets are higher for higher incomes. A person who makes over $200,000 a year is in the 40% income tax bracket.

Index Fund: A fund that matches some index, like the S&P 500, the Dow, or even the total stock market. The Vanguard company was a pioneer in developing index funds with low expenses.

Inflation: The increase in price of items in general. One easy way to understand inflation is to watch the prices of products that have been in existence for many years. For example, a Coke at a vending machine costs a dollar or more, yet that same product cost only ten cents forty years ago.

Initial Public Offering (IPO): The process that a company goes through to sell stocks, or ownership, to the public for the first time. Alternatively, it refers to a new issue. For example, if you hear a newsperson say, "The IPO jumped twenty points today," it means that the stock on its first day of trading went up twenty dollars per share.

Interest Payment: The payment made to the bondholder each year.

Interest Rate: The amount of money expressed as a percentage required to pay back a loan. For example, if the interest rate is 5%, and you take a one-year loan for $10,000, you'll have to pay back the $10,000 (this amount is called the principal) and an extra $500, the interest. A quick note: When you hear about the interest rate on television, they're usually referring to the *prime rate*.

Intrinsic Value: The real worth of a company. On the stock market, for example, the price of a stock is not the company's real worth. It's just the price that others have tagged on the stock. When the intrinsic value is significantly higher than the market value, a stock is described as undervalued. If the reverse is true, it's overvalued.

Investment Banks: This is an institution which helps corporations or governments issue stocks or bonds (this is called underwriting), but does not accept deposits, make loans, or perform any of the services that a commercial bank does.

Junk Bond: The least safe bond, but the one with the highest yield. Junk bonds may yield 14–15%. However, about one in twenty junk bonds defaults, meaning that bondholders get little or no money back.

Leverage: The use of other people's money. Some investors borrow to buy stock or futures contracts (for example, paying $1,000 for $2,000 worth of stocks). While this can potentially be very profitable, it also carries an equally large amount of risk.

Liabilities: Anything that takes money out of your pocket. Liabilities are almost always debts or taxes owed.

Limit Order: A type of stock order in which you specify the price you want to buy the stock at. Naturally, the price will be lower than the current price (nobody in their right mind wants to buy something for more than the market price). For example, if the current price is $60 per share for a stock, you might set a limit order at $50 per share, if you considered that a good price for the stock.

Liquid: Try to stick a spoon into a jar of honey. Now, try to put one into a glass of orange juice. With the glass of juice, it's much easier to put the spoon in and take the spoon out. The same is true in "liquid" markets. If there are a lot of orders to buy and sell, it's easy to buy and sell quickly at the price you want, even if you are trading large numbers of shares.

Market Capitalization (Market Cap): The total number of shares multiplied by the price per share. For example, the market capitalization of a stock that trades at $50 per share and has 10 million shares is $500 million. Stocks are often divided into three categories: Large capitalization (large cap), middle capitalization (mid cap), and small capitalization (small cap). Large cap stocks have a capitalization over $1 billion, and small caps have capitalizations under $200 million. Mid caps are somewhere in between.

Market Order: An order to buy at the market price. For a seller, the market price is the bid price, or the highest price somebody is willing to pay. For a buyer, the market price is the ask price, the highest price somebody is willing to sell their stock at. For example, if there is a $50 per share bid price and a $51 ask price, a market order to buy would be executed at $51 per share. A market order to sell would be executed at $50 per share.

Maturity: When applied to certificates of deposit, it refers to the length of time you must keep your money tied up in the CD before you can remove it. If you decide to remove your money earlier, you have to pay a fee.

Merger: When a company purchases another company of nearly the same size or slightly smaller. For example, when Daimler-Benz (makers of the Mercedes-Benz) purchased Chrysler, it was considered a merger, because the two companies were both so large. Many times, mergers are done to give the combined company access to a larger market and more profit by removing competition. That's why the government carefully scrutinizes large mergers.

Municipal Bonds: Tax-free state or local government bonds. In order to attract investors to buy bonds that fund state projects like dams or parks, the state government offers an incentive: The interest earned on the bonds is tax-free, whereas the earnings on any other type of bond are taxed as income.

Mutual Fund: A pool of money run by a *fund manager*. It's as if you and a group of your friends got together, pooled your money, and decided to give it to one person who you thought was good at investing. You agreed to pay him a percentage of the profits for running the money. A mutual fund is this scenario played out on a larger scale. FYI: The largest mutual fund company, Fidelity Investments, manages more than $300 billion.

NASDAQ (National Association of Securities Dealers Advanced Quotation System): A modern stock exchange that houses many technology companies, including Microsoft and Intel. NASDAQ is *far more* computerized than the NYSE, with most of the transactions pairing buyers and sellers done through computers.

NASDAQ Composite: An index that includes every stock on the NASDAQ. In a composite like the NASDAQ, stocks are weighted by their size. In other words, if a huge stock like Microsoft moves up three points, the composite is much more likely to close up for the day than if a small electrical company moves up three points. Remember: Size does matter.

Net Worth: This usually refers to a person's monetary value, but it's the same thing as *equity*. It's assets minus liabilities. For example, if a person owns stock worth $1 million and has debts of $400,000, their net worth is $600,000.

New York Stock Exchange (NYSE): The oldest stock exchange in the United States. It began in 1792 with the Buttonwood Agreement, in which twenty-four traders decided to trade stocks. The terminology still remains: To become a member and trade securities on the floor, you have to "buy a seat." In the beginning of the exchange, that meant actually buying a chair to sit on. Today, it costs over $1 million, and you receive a two foot by ten foot booth to do your paperwork (plus, of course, membership).

Options: The right, but not the obligation, to buy (for a call option) or sell (for a put option) a certain number of shares of a specific stock in a specified period of time. These options have a price tag and are often traded like merchandise. The other class of option is given to employees as a financial incentive and cannot be traded.

Partnership: A business entity composed of two or more people.

Points: Dollar-per-share movements in a stock. It's easier to say that a stock "dropped two points today" than it is to say, "The stock fell two dollars per share today," but they both mean the same thing.

Portfolio: Your investments. If you're a model, you may have a portfolio of pictures that you show to directors. If you're an investor, you have a group of investments, including stocks, bonds, and even bank accounts.

Price-to-Earnings Ratio (P/E): This is the price of the stock divided by the earnings per share (EPS). It's also called the valuation. For example, if the price of a stock is $20 and earnings are $2 per share, then the P/E ratio is 10.

Profit Margins: Net profit after taxes divided by sales, expressed as a percentage. If a company makes $1 million in profits and has revenues (sales) of $100 million, its profit margin is 1%. Higher profit margins are a mark of dominance in an industry.

Proxy Vote: Your vote as a shareholder in a company. If you can't be at the shareholder's meeting, you get a ballot to vote for stock splits or elect company directors. You get one vote per share. That ensures that key decisions are really made by those who own large numbers of shares, not small investors. Sorry.

Quote: The most current price. A price quote for a stock changes rapidly.

Real-Time Quote: A price quote that's in sync with the price on the exchange. Many times, quotes are delayed twenty minutes or more.

Real-time quotes are up to the second, so it's like being on the floor of the exchange.

Recession: A down period in the economy. Recessions can last anywhere from months to several years. When they drag on several years, they're better known as depressions (a common example of this was the Great Depression that lasted from 1929 to 1932).

Return on Equity (ROE): A company's earnings divided by its equity. For example, if the company has $100 million in equity and it earns $20 million, its ROE is 20%. ROE is a measure of how well a company is using what it already has—assets—to produce income—earnings.

Return on Investment (ROI): Also known as yield. This is the amount of money you make divided by the amount of money you invest. In other words, say you decide to invest $1,000 in a company beginning in January of 2001. In January of 2002, you realize that you have $1,250. That means you made $250. And since you started with $1,000, you have $250 ÷ $1,000 which is .25, or 25%.

Risk: The idea that anything you do that gives you a chance of winning also involves a chance of loss. Investors are intelligent risk takers. For example, as an investor, you're betting that a company can increase the amount of money it makes each year. If this happens, you stand to make a good amount of money from your investments. But you're also risking the possibility that the earnings may take a hit or even that the company could go bankrupt.

Sell Short: The process of borrowing shares, selling them, and then hoping to buy them back at a lower price (buying to cover). While this is a somewhat advanced process that no young investor should be involved with, it's good to understand that it's a kind of reverse capitalism: "Sell high, buy low." For example, if you sell one hundred shares short at $10 per share, you have $1,000 in your account. However, you're obligated to buy back those shares. If the price goes down to $5 per share, you can buy back at $500 and pocket the remaining $500. If the price goes to $15 per share, you're in the hole for $500.

Share: Part ownership in a company. One share represents the *least* amount that you can own of a company. Think of shares as pieces of a pizza pie.

Shareholder: A person who owns shares in a company.

Social Security: A government program that gives people over the age of sixty-five a monthly stipend. Unfortunately, the government still takes a piece of everyone's paycheck for the Social Security fund to pay for this, but the government has made more withdrawals from the fund than deposits. It's expected to run out by 2029.

Sole Proprietorship: The total ownership of a company by one person. Small companies are usually sole proprietorships. While this type of company requires less of a paperwork hassle, if the company goes bankrupt, the owner is personally responsible for paying back his creditors. This means that he has to give up his most of his assets, including, for example, his car, to pay back the people he took loans from if his company can't pay them back.

Specialist: A person on an exchange who matches buy and sell orders for a given stock. On the NYSE, for example, there is one specialist per stock. The specialist keeps everything running smoothly.

Spin Off: When a company decides to separate a division, it's called a "spin off." The parent company will take the spin off company public, thereby raising a lot of cash for itself and that company.

Spread: The difference between the bid and ask price. A small difference, "a tight spread," is considered more fair for the average investor. For example, if the spread is 50 bid by 52 ask, a person could buy at 52 and then sell at 50. Clearly, this wouldn't be in their best interest. Thus, the stock would have to go up more than two points for the investor to make a profit. Smaller spreads are more desirable because the stock has to go up less before the investor can sell at a profit.

Standard and Poor's 500 (S&P 500): An index of five hundred major stocks ranked by Standard and Poor, a stock analysis company. The

S&P 500 is considered a benchmark for mutual fund managers, but the sad fact is that most of them cannot produce the returns that this index generates.

Stock Market: This is a general term for the trading of stocks through organized exchanges. Most of the emphasis is placed on two major exchanges: the Dow Jones Industrial Average (the Dow) and the NASDAQ.

Stock Market Index: A group of stocks that are used to track a broader market. For example, there are many indices that measure technology or Internet stocks. Say an index includes, for example, thirty stocks. The starting price may be $1000. If the stocks in that index go up on one day 2%, the index will register 1020. Indices just make it easier to track how a group is doing in general.

Stock Option: The right, but not the obligation, to buy or sell a stock at a certain price by a given date. You'll encounter stock options as part of a company's incentive plan to lure employees. For example, a company might decide that if I join their firm, I would receive 1,000 options. Say these options give me the right to buy the stock at $20 per share within the next three years. If the company's stock goes to $60, each option is worth $60, for a profit of $40 per option, and I've got a nice $40,000 windfall. But if in those three years the price of the stock falls to $5, I'm not going to exercise those options, so I don't make any profit.

Stocks: Financial devices that allow you to have part ownership in a company, receiving all the benefits of an owner, including dividend payments and the right to vote on key decisions. Also known as *equities*.

Stock Split: When the number of shares of a stock is increased and the price is decreased. Splits are a marketing gimmick to make the shares look cheaper and more attractive. Otherwise, splits do nothing to the company. The most common type of split is a 2-for-1 split. In this type of a split a company doubles the number of shares and cuts the price in half. For example, Microsoft may decide to announce a 2-for-1 split. It has 500 million shares and the price per share is $120. By splitting, the price falls to $60 per share, but the number of shares doubles to 1 billion. Note that the market capitalization remains the same.

Stop-Loss Order: An order to sell a stock at market when it hits a certain price. This type of order cuts losses short. For example, let's say I set up a stop-loss order at $55. The stock is at $60, but it falls to $57 then $56, then $55. When it hits $55, the order to sell at the market price (the bid price) is executed. As a result, I would've sold my stock at $55 per share even if the price continued to fall to $53 or $50 per share.

System Trading: Using a computer program to develop an efficient and profitable method of buying and selling stocks automatically. Computers have made prodigious amounts of data available at low cost, and these same instruments also have the number-crunching power to develop these trading strategies.

Tax Deduction: Expenses or a loss on investments that offsets taxable income.

Tax Exclusion: Income that a person or company makes that isn't taxable.

Tax Shelter: An investment, like *municipal bonds*, that offers tax benefits. For example, municipal bonds offer interest payments that aren't taxed as income, like normal bonds.

Technical Analysis: The use of charts and graphs to predict the price of a stock.

Ticker Symbol: The abbreviation for a stock. On Wall Street, you'll still see ticker machines that scroll stock prices. The abbreviated price makes it a lot easier to go through hundreds of companies relatively quickly.

Time Worth: My made-up term for a measure of a person's real wealth. It isn't how much his assets are worth, but *how long he could live without a paycheck every week*. If he could quit work and live comfortably for a long time, then that's a high time worth.

Unrealized Gain: When you make a gain on an investment like a stock, and you don't sell that stock and cash out your profit, it's an unrealized gain. Unrealized gains aren't taxed until you cash out.

Value (of a bond): All bonds have an initial price called the "par value." For example, a bond may have a value of $100. If that bond yields 10%, you receive $10 a year (of course, you could own many of these bonds, allowing you to earn more than just $10 a year). That $10 a year always stays the same, but the value of the bond fluctuates. For example, the value may fall to $50. Receiving $10 a year, the yield now becomes 20% ($10 ÷ $50). If the value rose to $200, the yield would be 5% ($10 ÷ $200). Nifty stuff, huh?

Venture Capitalist: A company that invests in young companies. By taking the risk of investing in the initial stages of a small company, venture capitalists stand to benefit massively if the company becomes successful. Venture capitalists who've invested in Apple, Microsoft, and Yahoo! have become legends in their industry.

Volume: The number of shares traded on the stock exchange. Today, the total volume of the New York Stock Exchange ranges in the hundreds of millions of shares.

Wall Street: The area in Manhattan that's home to the New York Stock Exchange and a host of other financial exchanges and financial enterprises.

Wealth-building Return: A return on investment that is good enough to make you *very* wealthy over time. A minimum wealth-building return is 15% a year.

Yield: This is the same thing as return on investment, but it's usually tied to a bond. For example, a newsperson may say, "The yield on the thirty-year bond has fallen." Thus, the percentage rate of interest may have dropped from 6% to 5.5%.